Edward G. Porter

**The Beginning of the Revolution**

Edward G. Porter

**The Beginning of the Revolution**

ISBN/EAN: 9783337234485

Printed in Europe, USA, Canada, Australia, Japan

Cover: Foto ©Andreas Hilbeck / pixelio.de

More available books at **www.hansebooks.com**

# THE

# BEGINNING

OF

# THE REVOLUTION.

BY THE

REV. EDWARD G. PORTER, A. M.

REPRINTED FROM THE MEMORIAL HISTORY OF BOSTON.

BOSTON:

JAMES R. OSGOOD AND COMPANY.

1882.

# THE

# MEMORIAL HISTORY OF BOSTON.

## The Revolutionary Period.

## CHAPTER I.

### THE BEGINNING OF THE REVOLUTION.

BY THE REV. EDWARD G. PORTER,

*Pastor of the Hancock Church, Lexington.*

WHATEVER period we fix upon as the beginning of the American Revolution, we are sure to find some preceding event which, in a greater or less degree, might justly claim recognition on that account. It has generally been conceded that the war opened with the outbreak of hostilities on the morning of April 19, 1775: and that opinion will probably never be reversed. But as there were reformers before the Reformation, so there were many public acts in the Province deemed revolutionary before the memorable engagement on Lexington Common. Blood had been previously shed in a collision between the king's troops and American citizens in the streets of Boston. Remonstrances against the arbitrary measures of the British Government had repeatedly taken the shape of open and defiant resistance. The Congress of 1765 had issued a Declaration of Rights which, though accompanied by expressions of loyalty to the king, was a very pronounced step towards colonial union and independence. The utterances of Franklin, of Otis, and of Samuel Adams, and the favor with which they were received, clearly indicated the ardent aspirations of the people for political liberty. Every successive encroachment of the Crown was met by an immediate and determined protest. For years the public mind had been in a state of such chronic agitation that the peace was at any time liable to be disturbed by acts of violence.

It is greatly to the credit of the colonists, as British subjects, that the final rupture was so long in coming. They would certainly have been justified in the judgment of mankind had they precipitated rebellion in the

earlier stages of their oppression  When we remember what indignities
had been heaped upon them ever since the abrogation of the charter in
1684; when we recall the sufferings to which they were subjected by the
passage of the numerous navigation laws restricting their commerce and
prostrating their industries; when we bear in mind that the affection, which
for a century and a half the colonists sincerely cherished for the mother
country, was never cordially reciprocated,—we are not surprised that a feeling of estrangement at last grew up among them.  The wonder is that it
did not assert itself long before.  For, be it remembered, the spirit of freedom which took up arms in 1775 was not a sudden development nor an
accidental discovery.  The people had always had it.  They brought it with
them from the Old World, where, from the days of King John, it had been
the birthright of the English race.[1]

And so the Revolution, when it came, was only the assertion of this old
principle,—a fundamental principle with the colonists, and one which they
had never surrendered.  Under its guidance they had repeatedly engaged in
acts which they considered lawful and patriotic, but which the officers of
government condemned as refractory, rebellious, or treasonable.  These
public acts, extending through many years, constitute no unimportant part
of our history, since they contributed largely to bring about the final issue,
and, by their close relation to subsequent events, belong to the Revolutionary period.

The excitement in Boston during the winter of 1760-61, connected with
the application of officers of the customs for writs of assistance in searching
houses for contraband goods, must ever be regarded as one of the most
important of the early movements foreshadowing the approaching conflict.
To understand the bearing of this event, it is necessary to take a glance at
the condition of political affairs at that time.

George III. had just come to the throne.  Canada had been conquered
from the French.  England, flushed with victory, was yet oppressed with a
heavy debt; and the attention of her ministers was turned to the system of
colonial administration with a view to a large increase of the revenue.  The
Colonies came out of the war with many losses, to be sure, but trained and
strengthened by hardship, encouraged by success, and eager to return to
the pursuits of peace.  The population was increasing; new and valuable
lands were occupied; and business began to revive with extraordinary
rapidity.

From this period we can distinctly trace the growth of two opposing
political principles, both of which had existed in New England side by
side from the very beginning with only an occasional clashing, but which
now were destined to contend with each other in an irrepressible conflict.

---

[1] [The development of the spirit is more ad-  outcome of independence was not faced seriously
mirably traced than elsewhere in Richard Froth-  till quite late.  For references in this matter see
ingham's *Rise of the Republic*.  The inevitable  Winsor's *Handbook*, p. 102. — ED.]

These principles found expression in the two parties long existing,[1] but which now began to draw apart more and more; namely, the party of freedom, and the party of prerogative, — the former insisting upon the right of self-government under the Crown, and the latter maintaining the authority of the Crown in the place of self-government. The question at issue was a radical one, and upon it turned the whole history of the country.

Without stopping to discuss the weakness of England's position, the want of statesmanship in her councils, and the strange infatuation with which she pursued her fatal policy, we cannot overlook certain acts of trade which at this time were enforced by the Court of Admiralty, and which were designed to make the enterprising commercial spirit of America tributary to Great Britain. Much of the mischief brought upon the Colonies can be traced to the Board of Trade, — a powerful organization devised originally by Charles II. and re-established by William III. to regulate the national and colonial commerce. Though only an advisory council, having no executive power, its influence with the king and ministry was such that its recommendations were usually adopted. Burke[2] speaks of this notable body as a kind of political "job, a sort of gently-ripening hot-house, where eight members of Parliament receive salaries of a thousand a year for a certain given time, in order to mature, at a proper season, a claim to two thousand." The Board was intended to make the Colonies "auxiliary to English trade. The Englishman in America was to be employed in making the fortune of the Englishman at home."[3]

At the time of which we are now speaking, a profitable though illicit trade had sprung up between the northern colonies and the West Indies. Instructions were sent to the colonial governors to put a stop to this trade. Francis Bernard, late Governor of New Jersey, and a well known friend of British authority, having succeeded Pownall as Governor of Massachusetts, informed the Legislature in a speech shortly after his arrival "that they derived blessings from their subjection to Great Britain." The Council, in a carefully worded reply, joined in acknowledging the "happiness of the times," but instead of recognizing their "subjection," they spoke only of their "relation" to Great Britain; and the House, weighing also its words, spoke of "the connection between the mother country and the provinces on the principles of filial obedience, protection, and justice."[4] An opportunity soon occurred to show that the difference in language between the Royal Governor and the General Court was a deep-seated difference of principle and of purpose.

For many years the custom-house officers had availed themselves of their position to accumulate large sums, especially from a misuse of forfeit-

---

[1] [They were exemplified in the long struggle for the maintenance of the first charter (see Mr. Deane's chapter in Vol. I), and in the conflict over the royal governors' salaries subsequently (see Dr. Ellis's chapter in Vol. II). — ED.]

[2] *Speech on the Economical Reform.*

[3] Palfrey, *History of New England*, vol. iv. p. 24.

[4] Barry, *Hist. of Mass.* ii. 256; Bancroft, iv. 378; and Dr. Ellis's chapter in Vol. II. of this History.

ures under the old Sugar Act of 1733. This practice, added to the official
rigor and party spirit with which they enforced the commercial laws, led to
a general and deep-seated feeling of antipathy towards them on the part
of the merchants.[1] This antipathy was greatly aggravated by a decision in
the Superior Court against the treasurer of the Province, and in support of
the attitude of the officers of customs.[2]

In November, 1760, Charles Paxton,[3] who was the head of the customs
in Boston, instructed a deputy in Salem to petition the Court for "writs of
assistance," to enable them forcibly
to enter dwelling-houses and warehouses in the execution of
their duty. Exceptions were
at once taken to this applica-
tion, and a hearing was asked for by James Otis, an ardent young patriot,
whose connection with this case forms one of the most brilliant chapters in
our history. At the first agitation of the question he held the post of
advocate-general for the Colony, but rather than act for the Crown he had
resigned the position. "This is the opening scene of American resistance.[4]
It began in New England, and made its first battle-ground in a court-room.
A lawyer of Boston, with a tongue of flame and the inspiration of a seer,
stepped forward to demonstrate that all arbitrary authority was unconstitutional and against the law."[5] The trial came on in February, 1761. Thomas
Hutchinson, who had just succeeded Stephen Sewall as chief-justice, sat
with his four associates, "with voluminous wigs, broad bands, and robes of
scarlet cloth," in the crowded council chamber of the old Boston town house,
"an imposing and elegant apartment, ornamented with two splendid full-
length portraits of Charles II. and James II." The case was opened for the
Crown by Jeremiah Gridley as the king's attorney, and the validity of writs
of assistance was maintained by an appeal to statute law and to English
practice. Oxenbridge Thacher calmly replied with much legal and technical
ability, claiming that the rule in English courts was not applicable in this
case to America. James Otis[6] now appeared for the inhabitants of Boston,
and in an impassioned speech of over four hours in length he swayed both
the court and the crowded audience with marvellous power. He said: —

---

[1] A petition was sent to the General Court
at this time, charging the officers of the Crown
with appropriating to their own use moneys belonging to the Province. This petition was
signed by over fifty leading merchants, whose
names may be found in Drake's *Hist. of Boston*,
657, *note*.

[2] Hutchinson, *Massachusetts Bay*, iii. 89–92;
Minot, *Hist. of Mass.*, ii. 80–87; Barry, 262, 263.

[3] [There is a portrait of Paxton in the
Mass. Hist. Society's gallery. One, supposed to
be by Copley, is in the American Antiqua-
rian Society at Worcester. It is not recognized
by Perkins. — ED.]

[4] John Adams to the Abbé Mably. *Works*,
v. 492.

[5] Bancroft, iv. 414.

[6] This eloquent champion of liberty was a
native of Barnstable, and a graduate of Harvard in 1743. He began the practice of law at
Plymouth, but two years later removed to Boston,
where he rose to distinction as an earnest advocate of his country's rights. His father, the elder
Otis, was a distinguished politician and Speaker
of the House, and a candidate for the vacant
judgeship which Governor Bernard had given to
Hutchinson. See Tudor's *Life of Otis*; Hutchinson, iii. 86, *et seq.*; Barry, pp. 258–259.

"I am determined, to my dying day, to oppose, with all the powers and faculties God has given me, all such instruments, of slavery on the one hand and villany on the other, as this writ of assistance is. . . . I argue in favor of British liberties at a time when we hear the greatest monarch upon earth declaring from his throne that he glories in the name of Briton, and that the privileges of his people are dearer to him than the most valuable prerogatives of the Crown. I oppose that kind of power the exercise of which, in former periods of English history, cost one King of England his head and another his throne."

Otis then proceeded to argue that while special writs might be legal, the present writ, being general, was illegal. Any one with this writ might be a tyrant. Again, he said, this writ was perpetual. There was to be no return, and whoever executed it was responsible to no one for his doings. He might reign secure in his petty tyranny, and spread terror and desolation around him. The writ was also unlimited. Officers might enter all houses at will, and command all to assist them; and even menial servants might enforce its provisions. He said : —

"Now the freedom of one's house is an essential branch of English liberty. A man's house is his castle; and while he is quiet, he is as well guarded as a prince. This writ, if declared legal, totally annihilates this privilege. Custom-house officers might enter our houses when they please, and we could not resist them. Upon bare suspicion they could exercise this wanton power. . . . Both reason and the Constitution are against this writ. The only authority that can be found for it is a law enacted in the zenith of arbitrary power, when, in the reign of Charles II., Star Chamber powers were pushed to extremity by some ignorant clerk of the exchequer. But even if the writ could be elsewhere found, it would still be illegal. All precedents are under the control of the principles of law. . . . No acts of Parliament can establish such a writ. Though it should be made in the very words of the petition it would be void, for every act against the Constitution is void." [1]

Notwithstanding this forcible argument, and the soul-stirring eloquence with which it was presented, it did not prevail. The older members of the

[1] It is greatly to be regretted that this celebrated speech, which, in the judgment of many, originated the party of Revolution in Massachusetts, was never committed to writing. For such fragments of it as we have we are indebted to a few notes taken at the time, and to some incidental allusions found in letters of Bernard and Hutchinson. John Adams, late in life, "after a lapse of fifty-seven years," wrote out, by request, as much as he could remember of the argument of the speech. See Minot, ii. 91-99; Tudor's *Life of Otis*; Bancroft, iv. 416, note; Correspondence of John Adams and Mrs. Warren in 5 *Mass. Hist. Coll.* iv. 340; *Essex Inst. Hist. Coll.* Aug. 1869; Adams's *Life and Works of John Adams*, i. 59, 81, 82; ii. 124, 523, 524. [The case can be studied from a contemporary point of view in the reports made by the Josiah Quincy of that day, of cases in the Massachusetts Superior Court, 1761-1772, which were published in 1865, edited by his great-grandson General Samuel M. Quincy, with an appendix on the writs of assistance by Horace Gray, the present Chief-Justice of the Commonwealth. The late Horace Binney of Philadelphia wrote of the book, at the time, to Miss E. S. Quincy: "I have now read the reports, and with great satisfaction. They had good law in Massachusetts in the days of your grandfather, as well as good lawyers and a good reporter. Mr. Gray's appendix is one of the most clear, accurate, and exhaustive expositions that I have ever read, and has brought me much better instruction than I had before. I rather think they were legal under the act of Parliament, but I cannot believe they were constitutional, either here or in England, except as anything an act of Parliament does is constitutional." — ED.]

court were favorably disposed; but they yielded to the solicitations of Hutchinson, who proposed to continue the cause to the next term, in order, meanwhile, to apply to England for definite instructions. In due time the

*James Otis*[1]

answer came, in support of his well known position; and the court, with the semblance of authority rather than law, decided that the writs of assistance should be granted whenever the revenue officers applied for them.[2]

[1] [This cut follows a painting by Blackburn, in 1755, now owned by Mrs. Henry Darwin Rogers, by whose permission it is here copied. Having been more than once before engraved (see A. B. Durand's in Tudor's *Life of Otis*; another by J. R. Smith; and a poor one in Loring's *Hundred Boston Orators*), it was admirably put on steel by Schlecht, in 1870, for Bryant and Gay's *United States*, iii. 332. There is a genealogy of the Otis family in *N. E. Hist. and Geneal. Reg.* iv. and v.; also see Freeman's *History of Cape Cod*. Otis at one time lived where the Adams Express Company's building on Court Street now is. No American has received a more splendid memorial than Crawford has bestowed on Otis in the statue in the chapel at Mount Auburn. See an estimate of Otis in Mr. Goddard's chapter in the present volume. — ED.]

[2] Hutchinson, iii. 96; Bancroft, iv. 418; Barry, p. 267.

But Thacher and Otis had not spoken in vain.[1] They had electrified the people, and scattered the seeds which soon germinated in a spirit of combined resistance against the encroachments of unlawful power. Among those attending the court was the youthful John Adams, who had just been admitted as a barrister, and whose soul was ready to receive the patriotic fire from the lips of Otis. "It was to Mr. Adams like the oath of Hamilcar administered to Hannibal. It is doubtful whether Otis himself, or any person of his auditory, perceived or imagined the consequences which were to flow from the principles developed in that argument."[2] Patriots were created by it on the spot, — men who awoke that day as from a sleep, and shook themselves for action. Every one felt that a crisis was approaching in the affairs of the Province, if indeed it had not already come.

In tracing the causes which led to the final independence of America, it is always to be borne in mind that independence, in the political sense of the word, was not what the colonists originally desired. They were proud of their position as British subjects; and not until their loyalty had endured a long series of shocks, did it occur to any one that a separation was either possible or desirable. This will explain the docility with which the people of New England submitted to gross abuses and high-handed political measures through a period of over thirty years without doing more than to assert their rights, and to seek peaceable means of redress. They loved the mother country, and rejoiced in her prosperity.[3] Her history, her greatness, her triumphs, were all theirs. Their literature, their laws, their social life, their religious faith, were all English. Most of the towns and counties in Massachusetts were named after those in England, showing the affection the colonists had for the country from which they came. The architecture of Boston houses was almost an exact reproduction of that which prevailed in London or Bristol. A relationship of blood, of affection, and of interest was maintained by the closest communication which that age afforded. Packets were continually plying between the two countries; personal and business correspondence was frequent; and, in ordinary times, this intimacy was not affected by the official character and conduct of those who represented British authority on these shores. If the exercise of that authority had not exceeded its just limits, it would certainly have been a long time before the colonists would have demanded or accepted anything like a political separation. They were not adventurers, seeking capital out of conflict, but peaceable, industrious, law-abiding citizens; asking only for equality with their fellow-subjects, and deliverance from special and unequal legislation. They knew their rights under the charter, and were resolved to maintain them; and in this they were simply true to the traditions of the Anglo-Saxon race

---

[1] [The lawyers engaged in this cause are characterized in the chapter in Vol. IV. by Mr. John T. Morse, Jr. — EDS.]

[2] C. F. Adams's *Life of John Adams*, i. 81.
[3] Greene, *Historical View of the American Revolution*, pp. 5, 6.

from which they sprang. Their lot was cast in troublous times, but the trouble was not of their fomenting. They never invoked revolution, but were driven to it at last against their will by the stern logic of events. One of these events has already been described; but properly speaking, the great struggle did not begin with the excitement attending the application for writs of assistance. That excitement did not affect the country at large, nor did it seriously disturb the loyalty of the people of Boston. It led to much discussion and speculation, but to no organized resistance.

The first direct occasion for the uprising in America was the attempt on the part of the British Government to raise a revenue from the Colonies without their consent and without a representation in Parliament. Upon this turned the whole controversy, which lasted more than ten years and terminated in the final appeal to arms.

After the Peace of Paris,[1] England took a position of undisputed supremacy among the great powers of Europe. Her political and diplomatic influence was greatly increased by her military successes and her new territorial acquisitions. But this pre-eminence was attended by an exhausted treasury, and the first important question for her statesmen to ask was, how to increase the revenue. The American colonies, it was known, were gaining rapidly in population and wealth. There was no doubt of their ability to furnish large sums to the Crown. The people were loyal, and would be likely to sustain further draughts upon their resources.

So reasoned Charles Townshend, first lord of trade and secretary for the colonies in the new ministry formed by the Earl of Bute. No sooner did Townshend take office than he was ready with his audacious scheme to ignore charters, precedents, laws, and honor; to abrogate the rights and privileges of colonial legislatures; and to give Parliament absolute authority to tax an unwilling people to whom the privilege of representation had never been granted.

Townshend's scheme, in the form in which he presented it, did not succeed; but shortly after, — in March, 1763, — Grenville, first lord of the admiralty, eager to advance the interests of British trade, brought in a bill "for the further improvement of his majesty's revenue of the customs," authorizing naval officers on the American coast to act as custom-house officers. This bill soon passed both Houses and became a law.[2]

Bute's ministry was of short duration. Grenville soon took his place, supported by Egremont and Halifax, and retaining Jenkinson as principal secretary of the treasury. This triumvirate ministry was so unpopular as to become a "general joke;"[3] and was called "the three Horatii," "the

---

[1] Signed in February, 1763.

[2] Bancroft, v., 92; Barry, ii. 278.

[3] Walpole to Mann, April 30, 1763. See Lord Mahon (Stanhope), *History of England*, xli.

Athanasian administration," a "sort of Cerberus," a "three-headed monster, quieted by being gorged with patronage and office."[1]

One of Grenville's earliest measures was a bill for enforcing the Navigation Acts, in which he met with no opposition from Parliament or the King. His next plan was to provide for the army in America by taxing the Colonies. Upon this matter he consulted the board of trade, to ascertain " in what mode least burdensome and most palatable to the Colonies they can contribute toward the support of the additional expense which must attend their civil and military establishment."[2] The head of the board of trade was now the young Earl of Shelburne, an Irish peer, who was beginning to have great influence in British councils. On many questions he was a follower of Pitt, and was naturally opposed to extending the authority of Parliament. His reply gave no encouragement to the ministry; yet they continued pursuing their favorite project, and did all in their power to create a public sentiment in its favor. Before any action was taken Egremont died, and Shelburne was succeeded by the Earl of Hillsborough. Grenville now renewed his exertions for the passage of a revenue bill; and at a meeting of the lords of the treasury — Grenville, North, and Hunter — in Downing Street, on the morning of September 22, a minute was adopted directing their secretary, Jenkinson, " to write to the commissioners of the stamp duties to prepare a draught of a bill to be presented to Parliament for extending the stamp duties to the Colonies."[3] In obedience to this order the famous Stamp Act was prepared, and subsequently presented to Parliament. Probably its origin is not due to any one man. Bute thought of it, Jenkinson elaborated it, North supported it, Grenville demanded it, and England accepted it. It has generally been called, and with good reason, Grenville's measure. Whatever of credit or of odium attaches to it must be given to him. He did not expect the favor of the Colonies, but he was anxious to secure support at home; and as there was some doubt of the bill's passing without an exciting debate, he did not press the matter at once. Hoping also, possibly, to conciliate the Colonies, he yielded to the urgent solicitations of some of their representatives[4] who maintained that the proposed stamp duty was " an internal tax," and therefore that it would be better to " wait till some sort of consent to it shall be given by the several assemblies, to prevent a tax of that nature from being levied without the consent of the Colonies."[5] And so, " out of tenderness to the Colonies," the bill was not brought in for a year.

Meanwhile the Administration succeeded in carrying a measure, April 5, 1764, imposing duties on various enumerated foreign commodities imported into America, and upon colonial products exported to any other

[1] Wilkes to Earl Temple, in *Grenville Papers*, ii. 81.

[2] Bancroft, v. 107.

[3] *Treasury Minutes*, Sept. 22, 1763; Jenkinson's Letter, Sept. 23, 1763; Bancroft, v. 151.

[4] Thomas Penn and William Allen, of Pennsylvania; and Richard Jackson, his own private secretary.

[5] *Grenville Correspondence*, ii. 303; *Massachusetts Gazette*, May 10, 1764; Bancroft, v. 183; Barry, p. 284; Fitzmaurice, *Life of William, Earl of Shelburne*, i. 318, 319.

place than Great Britain. A heavy duty was also laid upon molasses and sugar. To enforce the provisions of this bill, enlarged power was given to the vice-admiralty courts, and penalties under the act were made recoverable in these courts.[1]

The news of the passage of the Sugar Act stirred up an intense commotion in all the maritime towns of America; the merchants everywhere held meetings, adopted memorials to the assemblies, and sent protests to England. In Boston, James Otis prepared a *Statement of the Rights of the Colonies*, and Oxenbridge Thacher expressed similar views in a pamphlet entitled *Sentiments of a British-American*.[2] A committee — Otis, Cushing, Thacher, Gray, and Sheafe — was also appointed to correspond with the other Colonies; and circulars were sent out stating the dangers that menaced "their most essential rights," and desiring the "united assistance" of all to secure, if possible, a repeal of the obnoxious acts, and to "prevent a stamp act, or any other impositions and taxes, upon this and the other American provinces."[3]

The Legislature, which had been prorogued month after month by Governor Bernard, to impede its action, finally met in October. Letters were received from the agents in England, and an address to the King was prepared; but as it failed of acceptance with the Council, it gave place to a milder address to the House of Commons, stating the objections which had been urged against the Sugar Act, and praying for a further delay of the Stamp Act.[4]

With the year 1765 the long dreaded measure, which had come to be regarded as the very symbol of usurpation, came into effect. At the opening of Parliament in January, Grenville presented the American question as one of obedience to the authority of the kingdom; and shortly after, with the support of Townshend, Jenyns,[5] and others, he proposed a series of resolutions, fifty-five in number, embracing the details of the Stamp Act, — the essential feature being the requirement that all legal and business documents in the colonies should be written on printed or stamped paper, to be had only of the tax collectors. All offences under this act were to be tried in the admiralty courts, and the taxes were to be collected arbitrarily, without any trial by jury.

---

[1] Minot, ii. 155; Holmes, *Annals*, ii. 125, *et seq*; Barry, ii. 286.

[2] Both published in Boston, June, 1764. The General Court sent a letter of instructions to Mr. Mauduit, the agent of Massachusetts in London, expressing the state of feeling. "If all the Colonies," says the letter, "are to be taxed at pleasure, without any representation in Parliament, what will there be to distinguish them, in point of liberty, from the subjects of the most absolute prince? Every charter-privilege may be taken from us by an appendix to a money bill, which, it seems, by the rules on the other side of the water, must not at any rate be petitioned

against. To what purpose will opposition to any resolutions of the ministry be, if they are passed with such rapidity as to render it impossible for us to be acquainted with them before they have received the sanction of an act of Parliament? A people may be free and tolerably happy without a particular branch of trade; but without the privilege of assessing their own taxes, they can be neither." Minot, ii. 168-173; Bradford, i. 21, 22.

[3] Hutchinson, iii. 110; Minot, ii. 175.

[4] *Massachusetts Records; Journal House of Representatives*, 1764, p. 102.

[5] Bancroft, v. 231-234.

Grenville advocated his bill with many plausible arguments and explanations. He had evidently anticipated all the difficulties it would encounter in England, but he failed utterly to comprehend the situation it would create in America. As was expected, it passed in a full house, February 27, without serious opposition, obtaining a majority of five to one. Among those who spoke and voted against it the names of Jackson, Beckford, Conway, and Barré deserve especial mention, as they afterward received the thanks of the Province for their services.

Colonel Barré[1] will always be gratefully remembered by the American people in connection with this event. Townshend having said that the Colonies were planted by the care, nourished by the indulgence, and protected by the arms of England, Barré rose and said : —

"*They planted by your care.*' No ! your oppressions planted them in America. . . . *They nourished up by your indulgence.*' They grew by your neglect of them. . . . *They protected by your arms.*' They have nobly taken up arms in your defence. . . . And believe me, — remember I this day told you so, — the same spirit of freedom which actuated that people at first will accompany them still."[2]

"The sun of liberty is set," wrote Dr. Franklin to Mr. Thompson[3] the very night that the act was passed; "the Americans must light the lamps of industry and economy."

The news of the passage of the Stamp Act reached Boston in April, and produced immediate alarm and indignation throughout the province.[4] Massachusetts and Virginia — "the head and the heart of the Revolution" — were the first to denounce the act, and they were soon followed by New York and Pennsylvania and all the other colonies. The determination was everywhere expressed that the act should never be executed. Sober men resisted it, because they saw that it would block the wheels of trade, prevent exchanges of property, interfere with all industry, and undermine their liberties, which they were not prepared thus to surrender. The case would have been entirely different if the colonists had levied these stamp duties

---

[1] Isaac Barré was born, 1726, of a Huguenot family living in Ireland; graduated at Trinity College, Dublin; entered the army and served in the French war; was a warm friend of Wolfe,

*Isaac Barré*

and was wounded at Quebec. Through the influence of Lord Shelburne he entered Parliament in 1761, after the fall of Pitt's ministry. His speeches were spirited, and often aggressive and harsh. He denounced tyranny and corruption, and usually appealed to the moral sympathies of men. He had something of the vehement, fiery eloquence of Pitt, and was a debater to be feared. See article on "Colonel Barré and his Times," in *Macmillan's Magazine*, December, 1876. The town of Barre, in Massachusetts, which was first named for Hutchinson, was afterward named for Barré.

[2] [It was in his speech of Feb. 6, 1765, that Barré had called the opposing party in the colonies the "Sons of Liberty," and the name brought over was soon adopted by them. — ED.]

[3] Afterward secretary of the Continental Congress.

[4] [The act was at once issued in a pamphlet by Edes and Gill, then keeping their press on the site of the present Adams Express Company's office, in Court Street. See Snow's *Boston*, p. 298. For the feelings engendered, see Warren's letter, in Frothingham's *Life of Warren*; and John Adams's *Works*, iii. 465. — ED.]

upon themselves, through their own assemblies, as the American people have since freely done to meet the cost of war; or if they had been allowed a voice in the government which exercised this authority.

A STAMP.[1]

It was an important principle which they felt to be at stake, — a principle which had hitherto been maintained in their relations with the mother country, and which they could not now see violated without a distinct and determined resistance.

At this juncture the Legislature of Massachusetts, at the suggestion of Otis, proposed the calling of an American Congress, consisting of committees from each of the thirteen colonies, to meet at New York in October, "to consult together," and consider the matter of a "united representation to implore relief."

While the leaders of the people were thus taking counsel of one another in solemn deliberations as to the course to be pursued, the popular feeling against the act, and the officers appointed to execute it, ran high in Boston. An occasion soon occurred to show how the people felt upon this subject. The birthday of the Prince of Wales, in August, was kept as a holiday. Crowds assembled in the streets, shouting " Pitt [2] and liberty!" Andrew Oliver, brother-in-law of Hutchinson, having been appointed stamp distributer, it was proposed that he be hung in effigy; and two days later, August 14, the public saw suspended

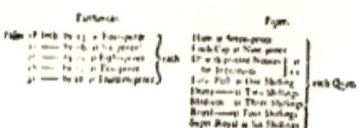

STAMP-OFFICE,
*Lincoln's-Inn,* 1765.

A

TABLE

Of the Prices of Parchment and Paper for the Service of America.

Paper for Printing

from the old elm known as Liberty Tree [3] a stuffed figure of the obnoxious official, together with a grotesque caricature of Bute.[4] This pageant had

---

[1] [There are a number of these stamps in the cabinet of the Massachusetts Historical Society; but our engraving is cut from one lent by Dr. Samuel A. Green. The impression is on a blue soft paper, secured by a transverse bit of soft metal, with another square piece of paper bearing the royal monogram covering the metal on the reverse. The accompanying reduced *fac-simile* of a schedule of prices for stamps is from a copy of the *Broadside,* kindly loaned by Dr. Green. — ED.]

[2] A change had just taken place in the ministry, and Pitt had returned to office.

[3] [See the engraving in chapter iv. of the present volume, with *note.* This fourteenth of August became a memorable anniversary for the Sons of Liberty, who eight years later, 1773, celebrated it by a "festivity" on Roxbury Common. Drake, *Town of Roxbury,* p. 266. — ED.]

[4] A large bust, designed to represent Lord Bute, with a head and horns upon it. Bute had been frequently burned in effigy in England in

been prepared by a party of Boston mechanics,[1] called Sons of Liberty, who, prompted by the intense feeling of the hour, devised this method of expressing it. Great excitement followed, and thousands assembled to view the spectacle. When the news reached Hutchinson he ordered the sheriff to remove the effigies; but nothing was done until evening, when they were taken down by those with whom the proceedings originated, and carried in procession, escorted by a great concourse of people, through the street, into the Old State House, and under the council chamber where Bernard,

*Boston Feb[y] 13.[th] 1766*

*Gentlemen*

*Your Humble Servants*

*The Sons of Liberty*[2]

Hutchinson, and their advisers were assembled. "Liberty, Property, and no Stamps!" was the shout which greeted the ears of those dignitaries. After repeated huzzas, the populace moved on to Kilby Street, where they destroyed a frame which the stamp distributer was said to be building for an office. Taking a portion of it, they proceeded to Fort Hill where Oliver lived, and burned the effigies in a bonfire before his house. Boston had

the guise of a jack-boot, — a pun upon his name as John, Earl of Bute. Bonfires of the jack-boot were repeated during several years both in England and America. Mahon (Stanhope), *History of England*, v. 25. [One of the most considerate of the English writers is Grahame, *History of the United States*, iv. 183. See Winsor's *Handbook*, p. 4, for other references. — ED.]

[1] Benjamin Edes, printer; Thomas Crafts,

painter; John Smith and Stephen Cleverly, braziers; John Avery, Jr., Thomas Chase, Henry Bass, and Henry Welles.

[2] [Subscription to a paper sent by the Order in Boston to the Sons of Liberty in New Hampshire, preserved in the *Belknap Papers*, iii., in the cabinet of the Massachusetts Historical Society. A silver punch-bowl, said to have been used by the Sons of Liberty, bought by William Mackay after the Revolution, and now owned by R. C. Mackay, was lately exhibited in the Old South Loan Collection. — ED.]

rarely witnessed such a scene. No one knew what would come of it. Bernard and Hutchinson took refuge in the Castle. The next day a proclamation was issued by the Governor, offering one hundred pounds reward to be paid upon the conviction of any person concerned in this transaction;[1] but no one cared to act as informant against such a strong current of popular feeling. A few days later, August 26, a mixed crowd collected near the Old State House, and proceeded to the house of the registrar of the admiralty, opposite the court house, and burned his public and private papers. They next plundered the house of the comptroller of customs, in Hanover Street, and then hurried to the mansion[2] of Lieut.-Governor Hutchinson, who had incurred the increasing dislike of the people in consequence of his subserviency to the Government, his greed of office, and his supposed influence in favor of the Stamp Act. Hutchinson and his family escaped; but the mob sacked his house and destroyed a large quantity of plate, pictures, clothing, books, and a valuable collection of manuscripts relating to the history of the colony.[3] This was a disgraceful proceeding, and would never have taken place but for the frenzy occasioned by the free use of liquor among the "roughs" who led on the mob.[4] A large public meeting was held the next morning in Faneuil Hall, and resolutions were passed strongly deprecating these lawless proceedings, and calling upon the selectmen to suppress such disorders in the future, and pledging the support of the inhabitants to preserve the peace.[5] That the leading Patriots had no sympathy whatever with this riotous outbreak is seen also in a letter written by Samuel Adams to Richard Jackson, the colonial agent in London, in which he denounced these proceedings as "high-handed outrages," of which the inhabitants, "within a few hours after the perpetration of the act, publicly declared their detestation. All was done the day following that could be expected from an orderly town, by whose influence a spirit

[1] Drake, *History of Boston*, p. 696.

[2] In Garden-court Street; taken down about 1830. See Introduction to Vol. II. p. xi.

[3] [Hutchinson, *Massachusetts Bay*, iii. 124; also see Introduction to Vol. I. of this History, p. xix, and Vol. II. p. 526; and Drake's *Landmarks*, p. 167. — ED.]

[4] [See contemporary accounts in Josiah Quincy's Diary, *Mass. Hist. Soc. Proc.*, April, 1858; and Joshua Henshaw's letter, in *N. E. Hist. and Geneal. Reg.*, July, 1878, p 268. Among the papers in the Charity Building is a copy of a deposition tending to show that the authorities had warning of the riot. Ebenezer Simpson testified to the selectmen that, Aug. 26, 1765, being at Spectacle Island, he met a man-of-war's boat, and one of the men told him that there was to be a mob in Boston that night, with intent to pull down the Lieut.-Governor's house, and that their ship's crew was sent for. Among these papers is also a copy of a letter from Warren to the selectmen, dated July 3,

1766, relative to the riot of the year before. He says he came into Boston about eight o'clock in the evening and overtook a much greater number of men than was usual, not in one large body but in little companies of four or five persons; and that the report of the disturbance being actually begun had already, at that time, reached Roxbury.

These papers also contain, as illustrating this period: a report on the condition of the North Battery in 1765, and estimates for rebuilding it in 1768; a report to the Governor on the population of Boston in 1765; and depositions as to trouble with British officers in 1768. These papers should be calendared. — ED.]

[5] [Drake's *Boston*, p. 701. There are on file in the city clerk's office various warning letters addressed to Benjamin Cudworth, deputy-sheriff, in a disguised hand; and also others to Stephen Greenleaf, sheriff, regarding Cudworth. They were read to the town, and pronounced "abusive." — ED.]

was raised to oppose and suppress it. It is possible these matters may be represented to our disadvantage, and therefore we desire you will take all possible opportunities to set them in a proper light."[1]

Throughout the colonies the same spirit of determined opposition to the Stamp Act was everywhere seen. Many of the officers appointed to distribute the stamps were compelled by the "unconquerable rage of the people" to resign, Oliver among the rest. Towns and legislatures hastened to make their declaration of rights, following o n e another "like a chime of bells," and planting themselves firmly upon the British Constitution and their chartered liberties. In the Massachusetts Assembly a series of fourteen resolves, p r e p a r e d by Samuel Adams, asserting the inherent and inalienable rights of the people, were particularly considered and passed in a full house.[2] These resolves met w i t h great favor, and were extensively published and quoted throughout t h e country.

OLIVER'S OATH.[3]

On October 7 the first American Congress ever held, composed of delegates from the different colonies, met in New York to take into consideration their rights, privileges, and grievances.[4] After mature deliberation in which members from all parts of the country participated, resolutions were passed embodying the warmest sentiments of loyalty to the King and respect for "that august body, the Parliament," and setting forth, in plain but temperate language, the reasonable demands of America, — such as the right to trial by jury, in opposition to the recent extension of the admiralty jurisdiction; and the right to freedom from taxation except through the colonial assemblies. The Congress also sent an address to the King, a memorial to the House of Lords, and a petition to the House of Commons. Before adjourning, this Congress consummated a virtual union by which the colonies became, as the delegates prophetically expressed it, "a bundle of sticks which could neither be bent nor broken."[5]

[1] Wells, *Life of Samuel Adams*, i. 63.

[2] Ibid., i. 74–77.

[3] [Mr. R. H. Dana, Jr., brought this oath to the attention of the Massachusetts Historical Society, in June, 1872, their *Proceedings* of that date showing a *facsimile* of it; the present is somewhat reduced. —ED.]

[4] [James Otis here showed his power of leadership. See Tudor's *Otis*; Bancroft, v.; Flanders's *Rutledge*; Ramsey's *South Carolina*. —ED.]

[5] Bancroft, v. 346. [This congress was a response to the call of Massachusetts. Its proceedings are in *Almon's Tracts*. —ED.]

In the mean time there had been further changes in the ministry, resulting in the elevation of the Rockingham Whigs to power. This announcement was received with great satisfaction, as it was understood that the new cabinet was more friendly to American claims. That this opinion had some foundation appears in the orders sent to the royal governors and to General Gage, commander of the forces at New York, only one week before the Stamp Act was to take effect, recommending " the utmost prudence and lenity," and advising a resort to " persuasive methods." [1]

When the first of November came, the people were prepared to prevent the execution of the odious act by refusing as one man to buy or use the stamps. In Boston they tolled the bells of the churches and fired minute-guns. Vessels in the harbor hung their flags at half-mast. " Liberty, Property, and no Stamps!" was the watchword passing everywhere from mouth to mouth. Effigies of Grenville and Huske [2] were suspended from Liberty Tree early in the morning, and in the afternoon were taken down and carried to the court house and to the North End, and then back to the gallows on the Neck, where they were hung for a short time, and afterward were cut down and torn to pieces. The crowd then quietly dispersed, and the night was entirely free from disturbance. [3]

As the Stamp Act had become a law, only stamped paper was legal; and as the people were firm in their determination not to use it, they were obliged to suspend business. The provincial courts were closed; marriages ceased; vessels were unmoored; and all commercial operations were paralyzed. Merchants in New York, Philadelphia, and Boston agreed not to import from England certain enumerated articles; and in general the people ceased using foreign luxuries, and turned their attention to domestic products. Frugality was the self-imposed order of the day, and it was not without its results.

In December a town-meeting was held in Boston, and a committee appointed to request of the Governor and Council that the courts might be opened. [4] At the opening of the Legislature in January, the House, in replying to the message of the Governor, demanded relief from the existing grievances. " The custom-houses are now open," they said, " and the people are permitted to transact their usual business. The courts of justice also must be opened, — opened immediately; and the law, the great rule of right, duly executed in every county in this province. This stopping of the course of justice is a grievance which this Court must inquire into. Justice must be fully administered without delay." [5] The Council laid this address upon the table; but, in an informal way, gave assurances that the courts

---

[1] *Massachusetts Gazette*, Feb. 6, 1766; *Debates in Parliament*, iv. 302-306.

[2] John Huske, a native of Portsmouth, N. H., who had removed to England and obtained a seat in the House of Commons, and taken a prominent part in favor of the Stamp Act.

[3] Drake, *Boston*, pp. 707, 708.

[4] This committee was composed of Samuel Adams, Thomas Cushing, John Hancock, Benjamin Kent, Samuel Sewall, John Rowe, Joshua Henshaw, and Arnold Welles; and they were authorized to employ Gridley, Otis, and John Adams as counsel. Diary of John Adams in *Works*, ii. 157, *et seq.*; Barry, p. 307.

[5] *Massachusetts Gazette*, Jan. 23, 1766; Hutchinson, iii. 143.

would be opened at the next term, and business allowed to be transacted as usual.

This bold attitude of the American people caused no little annoyance and anxiety to the Administration. The case was, moreover, complicated by the change of sentiment in England regarding the justice of the policy initiated by Grenville. The English people were not prepared to repudiate their own love of liberty, nor to force upon any of their fellow-subjects the measures of absolutism against which their own glorious history had been a standing protest. Especially were the commercial and manufacturing towns in England dissatisfied with this policy; for it had reacted most unfavorably upon them, interrupting trade, injuring credit, and creating much suffering and discontent. We are not surprised, therefore, to find that both sympathy and interest prompted the nation to urge the repeal of an act which was as hostile to their own welfare as to that of America.

Upon the reassembling of Parliament in January, 1766, the King, in his speech, stated that "matters of importance had happened in America, and orders had been issued for the support of lawful authority." [1] The Lords responded, as usual, in terms of deference and co-operation; but in the House of Commons, which was unusually full, a debate ensued such as perhaps had never been heard before within its walls. The venerable Pitt, after an absence of more than a year, had arrived in town that morning. Though in a very feeble condition, and suffering from the gout, he took his seat while the debate was in progress, and soon after rose and made his ever memorable speech, — a masterpiece of fiery eloquence in which he denounced the Stamp Act, and demanded its immediate repeal. He said : —

"It is now an act that has passed. I would speak with decency of every act of this House, but I must beg indulgence to speak of it with freedom. The subject of this debate is of greater importance than any that has ever engaged the attention of this House, — that subject only excepted when, nearly a century ago, it was a question whether you yourselves were to be bond or free. . . . On a question that may mortally wound the freedom of three millions of virtuous and brave subjects beyond the Atlantic Ocean, I cannot be silent."

He then proceeded to argue that as the colonies had never been really or virtually represented in Parliament, they could not be held " legally or constitutionally or reasonably subject to obedience to any money bill" of the kingdom. In replying to Grenville he said, a little later on : " The gentleman tells us America is obstinate ; America is almost in open rebellion ! I rejoice that America has resisted." Upon this the whole House started as if touched by an electric shock. Near the conclusion of his speech he said : —

"In a good cause, on a sound bottom, the force of this country can crush America to atoms. . . . But in such a cause your success would be hazardous. America, if she fell, would fall like the strong man ; she would embrace the pillars of the State,

[1] *Massachusetts Gazette*, March 27, 1766.

and pull down the Constitution along with her. . . . Upon the whole I will beg leave
to tell the House what is really my opinion. It is that the Stamp Act be repealed,
absolutely, totally, and immediately; that the reason for the repeal be assigned, because it was founded on an erroneous principle. . . ." [1]

Thus spoke the Great Commoner; with what effect upon the minds of
the House appeared in the current of sympathy which at once turned toward
him, and which, a little later on, expressed itself in the famous repeal.
Toward the last of the month the House resolved itself into a committee
of the whole to consider petitions for the repeal, which had been presented
by the merchants of London, Birmingham, Coventry, Bristol, Liverpool,
Manchester, and other towns. The sittings of this committee were continued more than two weeks. Among others, Benjamin Franklin, then a
colonial agent in London, was summoned to the bar of the House; and his
minute examination concerning the feelings and wishes of the Colonies contributed more to his personal fame than any previous occurrence in his life;
and it is doubtful whether he ever wrote or said anything abler than his ad-
mirable replies on this occasion. In all that he said he was prompt and
pertinent, accurate and concise, wise and true. The House of Commons
listened to him for ten days, and must have been as much astonished at his
answers as the whole American people were delighted with them.[2]

The committee who had listened to this remarkable examination soon
" reported that it was their opinion that the House be moved that leave be
given to bring in a bill to repeal the Stamp Act."

The crisis came on the night of February 21, when every seat was occupied, and the galleries, lobbies, and stairs were crowded with eager spectators. The debate was opened by Conway, one of the ministry, and a warm
friend of the Colonies. He was followed by Jenkinson, Burke, Grenville,

---

[1] Bancroft, v. 382-396; *Debates in Parliament,*
iv. 285-298.

[2] As a specimen of Franklin's shrewdness,
take a few of his answers: —

"*Question.* — Do you think it right that America should be protected by this country and pay
no part of the expense?

"*Answer.* — That is not the case. The Colonies raised, clothed, and paid during the last
war near twenty-five thousand men, and spent
many millions.

"*Q.* — Were you not reimbursed by Parliament?

"*A.* — . . . Only a very small part of what
we spent.

"*Q.* — Do you think the people of America
would submit to pay the stamp duty if it was
moderated?

"*A.* — No, never, unless compelled by force
of arms.

"*Q.* — What was the temper of America toward Great Britain before the year 1763?

"*A.* — The best in the world. . . .

"*Q.* — And what is their temper now?

"*A.* — Oh, very much altered.

"*Q.* — Did you ever hear the authority of
Parliament to make laws for America questioned
till lately?

"*A.* — The authority of Parliament was allowed to be valid in all laws except such as
should lay internal taxes. It was never disputed
in laying duties to regulate commerce.

"*Q.* — If the Stamp Act should be repealed,
and the Crown should make a requisition to the
Colonies for a sum of money, would they grant
it?

"*A.* — I believe they would.

"*Q.* — What used to be the pride of the
Americans?

"*A.* — To indulge in the fashions and manufactures of Great Britain.

"*Q.* — What is now their pride?

"*A.* — To wear their old clothes over again
till they can make new ones." — Bigelow, *Life of
Franklin,* i. 467-510; Sparks, *Franklin,* pp. 298-
300.

and Pitt. About half-past one in the morning the division took place, and Conway's bill of repeal was carried triumphantly by a vote of two hundred and seventy-five against one hundred and sixty-seven. Pitt and Conway were tumultuously applauded as they left the House, while Grenville [1] was greeted with hisses. The final debate on the repeal was still more decisive. In the Lords the bill was carried by a majority of thirty-four; and on the day following, March 17. it received the reluctant sanction of the King, who spoke of it as "a fatal compliance." London was delighted with the result; the church bells were rung merrily; ships displayed their colors; the streets were illuminated; and a public dinner was given by the friends of America. In Boston the news was received with every conceivable demonstration of joy.[2] Liberty Tree was decked with lanterns; bells and guns, flags and music, illuminations and fireworks, proclaimed in unmistakable language the gratitude and loyalty of the people.[3] New York voted statues to the King and to Pitt. Virginia voted a statue to the King, and South Carolina one to Pitt. Maryland passed a similar vote, and ordered a portrait of Lord Camden. Boston had previously voted letters of thanks to Barré and Conway, and requested their portraits for Faneuil Hall.[4]

In the outburst of joy at the repeal, the public mind had not considered the full meaning of the accompanying declaratory act[5] claiming for Parliament absolute power to bind America "in all cases whatsoever." This act was a fatal mistake, and a wanton blow at the well known American principle of local self-government; for it soon became evident that the object of Parliament was, after all, political subjugation. This was precisely the point upon which the colonists had taken their stand. It was not the mere pecuniary loss involved in the enforcement of the stamp tax that they were considering, — they were abundantly able to pay that, — but it was the underlying question of right; and if that were not conceded, it would soon be found

[1] Walpole, ii. 299, 300.

[2] [Speaker Cushing had enclosed, June 22, 1766, a letter of thanks to the king, and the *facsimile* on the next page is from Otis's letter to Cushing on this vote of thanks. The original is in the Lee papers in the University of Virginia Library. The principal demonstrations took place May 19, 1766. An obelisk was erected on the Common and decked with lanterns; Hancock illuminated his house and discharged fireworks in front of it from a stage; and these were responded to by similar demonstrations by the Sons of Liberty at the workhouse. Views of the obelisk were engraved by Revere, and one of them is given much reduced in Drake's *Landmarks*, p. 359. The earliest rumor of a repeal had appeared in the *Massachusetts Gazette*, April 3, 1766, having come from Philadelphia two days before. See Thornton's *Pulpit of the Revolution*, p. 120, where is also Chauncy's discourse on the repeal. — ED.]

[3] [A paper by General Gage concerning the Stamp Act and the revolutionary proceedings in Boston, is printed in *Mass. Hist. Coll.* iv. 367. There is in the collection of Charles P. Greenough, Esq., of Boston (whose treasures have been very generously put at my disposal, and from which I have often drawn in this and the final volume), a letter from London merchants to those of Boston, offering congratulations and encouragement on account of the repeal of the Stamp Act. A similar letter from business correspondents was contributed to the *Mass. Hist. Soc. Proc.*, March, 1876, p. 266, by Mr. T. C. Amory. — ED.]

[4] This was done at a town-meeting held Sept. 18, 1765. The portraits arrived in due time, and were hung in Faneuil Hall; but what became of them afterward is not known. They are supposed to have been removed when the British army had control of the town. Drake, pp. 703, 704. [See supplementary notes to the next chapter in this volume. — ED.]

[5] 6 George III. c. xii.

that the repeal was only a nominal and a temporary relief. Leading Patriots saw in this much to excite alarm; but for the time being, and for the sake of harmony, they were willing to remain silent.[1]

No well defined sentiment of union had as yet taken possession of the public mind. Not until it became evident that there was no other way of maintaining their freedom, did any of the Colonies think of measures tending to united action. One of the first to anticipate this necessity was Jonathan Mayhew, the patriotic pastor of the West Church in Boston, who, writing to his friend Otis one Lord's Day morning in June, 1766, said:—

"You have heard of the communion of churches; while I was thinking of this in my bed, the great use and importance of a communion of colonies appeared to me in a strong light. Would it not be decorous for our Assembly to send circulars to all the rest, expressing a desire to cement union among ourselves? A good

*Boston September 8th 1766.*

*I had yesterday the honor to prepare your votes in ye house of ... at a time when our Governor ... no more ... Poor suceeder, think ... never again have ... I heard the how to be*

*your most obedt humle servt*
*James Otis*

---

[1] Wells, *Life of Samuel Adams,* i. 116-118.

foundation for this has been laid by the Congress at New York ; never losing sight of
it may be the means of perpetuating our liberties." [1]

The possibility of such a union seems to have occurred to at least one
English statesman at this time ; for in the same month in which the above
words were penned we find Charles Townshend boldly advocating in the
House of Commons a radical measure aimed not only to secure a revenue,
but also to prevent any such accessions of strength as the Colonies might
gain by combined action. No man in the ministry was better informed
than Townshend upon American affairs. He knew the resources of the
people ; he anticipated their rapid development ; and the scheme which he
now promulgated was expressly devised to make the whole colonial power
tributary to the Crown. Therefore he favored the abolition of all their
charters ; and the substitution of a government in which the local assemblies should be restrained, a general congress forbidden, and the royal governors, judges, and attorneys become independent of the people.[2]

Townshend soon had further opportunities for prosecuting his scheme ;
for in the reconstruction of the ministry, which took place in the month of
July, he was selected as chancellor of the exchequer by the Duke of
Grafton, in the strangely incongruous ad-
ministration of Pitt, now created Earl of
Chatham. Townshend was the leading spirit
in the new government, and availed himself of every opportunity to urge the ad-
vantages of an American civil list. He
had been, with Grenville, a firm advocate of the Stamp Act. He ridiculed
the distinction between internal and external taxes. He insisted that
America should share the heavy financial burden of England.[3] In the absence of Chatham, who was most of the time suffering from feeble health,
he dictated to the ministry its colonial policy. " I would govern the
Americans," said he, " as subjects of Great Britain ; I would restrain their
trade and their manufactures as subordinate to the mother country.
These, our children, must not make themselves our allies in time of war
and our rivals in peace." With such purposes the resolute and reckless
chancellor pushed his way into favor with Parliament, ignoring the scruples
of his associates and defying the opposition of his enemies, until he succeeded in carrying the famous Townshend revenue bill through both
Houses, and obtained the royal assent. These acts levied a duty on glass,
paper, painters' colors, and tea ; established a board of customs at Boston
for collecting the whole American revenue ; and legalized writs of assistance.
The revenue was to be at the disposition of the King, and was to be chiefly
employed in the support of officers of the Crown, to secure their independence of the local legislatures. " The die is thrown ! " cried the Patriots of

[1] Bradford, *Life of Mawhew*, 428, 429. [See
also Mr. Goddard's chapter in the present volume. — ED.]

[2] Bancroft, vi. 9, 10.
[3] Fitzmaurice, *Life of William, Earl of Shelburne*, iii. 37 et seq.

Boston when they received the news of the passage of Townshend's bill: "the Rubicon is passed. . . . We will form an immediate and universal combination to eat nothing, drink nothing, wear nothing, imported from Great Britain. . . . Our strength consists in union; let us above all be of one heart and one mind ; let us call on our sister Colonies to join with us in asserting our rights."[1] Governor Bernard having refused a petition to summon the Legislature, a town-meeting was called Oct. 28, 1767; and the inhabitants voted neither to import nor to use certain articles of British production. A committee was appointed to obtain subscribers to such an agreement, and the resolutions were extensively circulated throughout the country. The newspapers took up the subject with great warmth, and aided in a very important degree the formation of public opinion at this critical period. Able writers contributed timely letters, among which those written by a " Farmer of Pennsylvania "[2] attained a very wide celebrity for their calm and vigorous treatment of the great constitutional questions of the day. The communications sent by the Massachusetts Legislature in January, 1768, to members of the Cabinet and to the provincial agent in London, contain the full argument respecting the claims of the colonies. These papers, as well as the petition to the king which accompanied them, and the circular-letter to the sister colonies which was issued shortly after, were all drafted by Samuel Adams, whose masterly grasp of the great political issues of the time attracted universal attention and gained a host of friends to the cause of liberty. The circular-letter just alluded to met with a very gratifying response from the other assemblies, and was a most efficient instrument in securing unity of purpose among the leaders of the people in all parts of the country. The publication of these important documents produced such an effect that the board of commissioners of the revenue immediately prepared a memorial to be sent to England, expressing apprehensions for their personal safety; complaining of the unwarrantable license of the American press,[3] of the non-importation league, and of New England town-meetings; and asking for assistance in the execution of the revenue laws; adding, that there was not a ship of war in the province, nor a company of soldiers nearer than New York.

This memorial, together with the reports of Bernard and Hutchinson, soon drew from Hillsborough, secretary for the colonies, an order sent to all the governors, bidding them use their influence with the assemblies to

---

[1] Barry, ii. 339.

[2] John Dickinson, afterward a member of the first Continental Congress. [To a letter of gratitude from Boston Dickinson returned a reply, which is preserved among the Charity Building papers, and is addressed "To the very respectable inhabitants of the town of Boston;" and expresses the "reverential gratitude" for the late letter received by him : —

PENNSYLVANIA, April 11, 1768.

The rank of the Town of Boston, the wisdom of her counsels, and the spirit of her conduct render, in my opin-

ion, the approbation of her inhabitants inestimable. . . . Love of my country engaged me in that attempt to vindicate her rights and assert her interests, which your generosity has thought proper so highly to applaud. . . . Never, until my heart becomes insensible of all worldly things, will it become insensible of the unspeakable obligations which, as an American, I owe to the inhabitants of the Province of Massachusetts Bay, for the vigilance with which they have watched over, and the magnanimity with which they have maintained, the liberties of the British colonies on this continent. A FARMER. — ED.]

[3] [See Mr. Goddard's chapter in this volume. — ED.]

take no notice of the "seditious" circular-letter, which was described as "of a most dangerous and factious tendency," calculated to inflame the minds of the people, to promote an illegal combination, and to excite open opposition to the authority of Parliament. The House of Representatives of Massachusetts was required, in His Majesty's name, to rescind their resolutions, and to "declare their disapprobation of the rash and hasty proceeding." In case of their refusal to comply, it was the King's pleasure that the Governor should immediately dissolve them.[1] At the same time General Gage, Commander-in-chief of the royal forces in America, was ordered to "strengthen the hands of the Government in the Province of the Massachusetts Bay, enforce a due obedience of the laws, and protect and support the civil magistrates and the officers of the Crown in the execution of their duty."[2] Further peremptory orders were sent to Gage, in June, to station a regiment permanently in Boston; and the admiralty was directed to send one frigate, two sloops, and two cutters to remain in Boston harbor; and Castle William was to be put in readiness for immediate use.[3]

For about a month previous to this the ship of war "Romney" had lain at anchor in the harbor, and her commander had occasioned much trouble by violently impressing New England seamen, and refusing to give them up, even when substitutes were offered. The excitement arising from this was increased by the seizure of the sloop "Liberty" (June 10, 1768), belonging to John Hancock, for an alleged false entry. The popular outbreak in consequence of these proceedings, though resulting in no serious injury, was magnified by the commissioners into an insurrection, and made the occasion of still further appeals for personal protection, by force of arms, in the discharge of their duties.[4] The citizens, in response to a call for a legal town-meeting to consider the matter, gathered in such numbers at Faneuil Hall that they were obliged to adjourn to the Old South Meeting-house, where, with Otis as moderator, an address to the Governor was unanimously voted, and a committee of twenty-one appointed to present it.[5] At an adjourned meeting the next day (June 15), Otis strongly recom-

---

[1] Hillsborough to Bernard, April 22, 1768.

[2] Hillsborough to Gage, April 23, 1768.

[3] [The annexed heliotypes follow originals made by the British engineers not far from this time, and issued with DesBarres's series of coast charts. One represents the harbor from Fort Hill; the other is a view of the town from Willis's Creek, in East Cambridge. — Ed.]

[4] [There is an account of this seizure in Drake's *Boston*, p. 736. See John Adams's *Works*, ii. 215. A prominent leader in the mob which endeavored to prevent the sloop from being towed under the guns of the "Romney" was a Boston tradesman, Daniel Malcolm, who had a year or two before some pretty sharp altercations with the revenue officers, accompanied with vigorous action, so that he was

found out to be not an easy person to deal with. The papers relating to these affairs of his are preserved among the Lee papers, in the libraries of Harvard College and the University of Virginia. Malcolm died shortly after, and they show his gravestone today in the Copp's Hill burying-ground, with its praises of him as "an enemy of oppression and one of the foremost in opposing the revenue acts on America;" and upon it are seen the bullet marks of the British soldiers, who used it as a target during the siege. Shurtleff's *Description of Boston*, p. 209. — Ed.]

[5] [This presentation took place at the Governor's house, on Jamaica Pond, where they were treated with wine, "which highly pleased [Bernard says] that part of them which had not been used to an interview with me." — Ed.]

mended peaceable and orderly methods of obtaining redress, and depre-
cated in the strongest terms all acts of mob violence, hoping that the
cause of their grievances would yet be removed; and added: "If not, and
we are called on to defend our liberties and privileges, I hope and believe
we shall, one and all, resist even unto blood; but I pray God Almighty
that this may never so happen." [1]

The Governor disclaimed having any responsibility for the occurrences
complained of, but promised to stop impressments. Meanwhile, Hillsborough's instructions to Massachusetts to rescind her non-importation resolutions arrived, and were communicated in a message from Bernard to the
General Court. Otis took the floor in reply, and spoke for two hours with
even more than his accustomed vehemence, showing that it would be impossible for this House to rescind a measure of the previous House which
had been already executed. He spoke respectfully of the King, but arraigned the course of the ministry and the legislation of Parliament with
great severity. The subject occupied the attention of the House for nine
days, under the guidance of a special committee.[2] The Governor communicated the threat to dissolve the Assembly in case they refused to
comply, and pressed them for a decision. A recess was requested for
consultation, but it was refused. The question was then put, in secret
session, whether the House would rescind the resolution "which gave birth
to their circular-letter to the several houses of representatives and burgesses
of the other colonies." The vote was taken *viva voce*, and stood ninety-
two nays against seventeen yeas. The answer to the Governor, informing
him of their decision, stated that they regarded the circular-letter moderate and innocent, respectful to Parliament, and dutiful to the King; that
they entertained sentiments of reverence and affection for both; that
they, as subjects, claimed the right of petition jointly and severally, of
correspondence, and of a free assembly; and that the charge of treason
was unjustly brought against them. The Governor, following his instructions, thereupon closed the session, and the next day dissolved the General
Court by proclamation. Thus was taken away the right of free discussion
vested in the time-honored representative Assembly of Massachusetts. It
was an act of arbitrary power, destined to recoil heavily upon those who
enforced it. The other Colonies felt that their liberties were invaded as
well, and sent the most cordial assurances of their sympathy and support.
In this we can clearly see a new impulse given to the sentiment of union as
a necessary means of mutual security. As dangers thickened, the people
stood more and more together, determined to assert and defend their constitutional rights against the unlawful aggressions of imperial power. It
soon became evident that the Administration had resolved upon employ-
ing the strong arm of military power to sustain its authority in the "re-

---

[1] *Boston News-Letter*, June 16 and 23, 1768.

[2] This committee consisted of Thomas Cushing (speaker), Mr. Otis, Samuel Adams (clerk),
John Hancock, Colonel Otis, Colonel Bowers,
Mr. Spooner, Colonel Warren, and Mr. Saun-
ders.

fractory" Province. Preparations were making to transfer two regiments from Halifax to Boston, and it was soon after announced that two others were expected from Ireland. This naturally led to a great excitement, and a town-meeting was called to consider what "wise, constitutional, loyal, and salutary measures" could be taken in the emergency. The Governor was requested to give information in regard to the troops, and to convene the Legislature. Upon his refusal, a convention of all the towns was proposed, to be held in Faneuil Hall within two weeks; and it was recommended that all the inhabitants should be provided with firearms and suitable ammunition;[1] and a day of fasting and prayer was appointed and observed in accordance with the New England custom.

The convention met on September 22, and was composed of representatives of nearly every settlement in the province. The same officers were chosen for chairman and clerk that filled those positions in the late Assembly, and the Governor was petitioned to "cause an assembly to be immediately convened." He refused to receive the petition, and denounced the convention as illegal, advising the members to separate at once, or they would "repent their rashness." The convention did not follow his advice, but continued in session six days, and reaffirmed the former declarations made by the General Court concerning their charter rights. The proceedings throughout were calm and moderate. A respectful petition to the king was prepared, in which they wholly disclaimed the charge of a rebellious spirit. An address to the people was also adopted, recommending submission to legal authority and abstinence from all participation in acts of violence. This was the first of those independent popular assemblies which soon began to exercise political power in the colonies. The Patriot leaders were wise and sagacious men, who, in asserting their rights, knew well how to keep the law on their side. When the proceedings of this convention were submitted to the attorney-general, and to the solicitor-general of England, to ascertain if they were treasonable, both declared that they were not. "Look into the papers," said De Grey, "and see how well these Americans are versed in the crown law. I doubt whether they have been guilty of an overt act of treason, but I am sure they have come within a hair's breadth of it."[2]

No sooner had the convention adjourned than the fleet arrived in the harbor, bringing two regiments, with artillery, under command of Colonel Dalrymple.[3] In response to a requisition for quarters in the town the council, and afterwards the selectmen, adhering to the law, declined to act, stating that the barracks at Castle Island were provided for that purpose.

[1] Hutchinson, iii. app. i.; *Boston News-Letter*, postscript, Sept. 22, 1768.

[2] Bancroft, vi. 206.

[3] [The Patriots had prepared to fire the beacon above the town, and had placed a broken tar barrel in the skillet. This was perhaps the only time in which the surrounding country came near being roused in this way. Governor Bernard was informed of the movement, and sent Sheriff Greenleaf to remove the combustibles. Frothingham, *Life of Warren*, p. 80. An excellent likeness of Greenleaf, by Smibert, is owned by Mrs. S. G. Bulfinch, of Cambridge. — Ed.]

On the first of October eight armed ships, with their tenders, approached the wharves, with cannon loaded and springs on the cables. The Fourteenth and Twenty-ninth regiments, and a part of the Fifty-ninth, with two field-pieces, landed at Long Wharf and marched with fixed bayonets, drums beating and colors flying, through the streets as far as the Common, where a portion of the troops encamped, the remainder being allowed by the Sons of Liberty, later in the day, to occupy Faneuil Hall.[1] We can easily imagine the surprise and indignation with which the people of Boston beheld this demonstration of authority. They keenly felt the insult offered to their loyalty, and though no open resistance was made it was soon apparent that such a state of things could only engender mutual hostility which might at any time break out in a disturbance of the peace. The odious terms "rebel" and "tyrant" were now spoken with increasing bitterness, and the lines were drawn more sharply than ever between Tory and Patriot. While Boston was thus in the hands of a hireling soldiery, her people waited anxiously for intelligence from abroad, hoping that their communications to the King and Parliament would meet with a favorable consideration;[2] but again they were doomed to disappointment. Changes had taken place in the cabinet, but there was no change in the purpose of the Government. Chatham had resigned; Shelburne was removed; and Lord North[3] had taken the place left vacant by the death of Townshend.[4] At the opening of Parliament, the King referred to Boston as being "in a state of disobedience to all law and government," and declared it to be his purpose "to defeat the mischievous designs of those turbulent and seditious persons" who had "but too successfully deluded numbers" of his subjects in America. An animated debate followed, in which it was said that the difficulties in governing Massachusetts were "insurmountable, unless its charter and laws should be so changed as to give the King the appointment of the council, and to the sheriffs the sole power of returning juries."

[1] [Paul Revere's plate, showing this landing, is given in Vol. II. p. 552. Mrs. Turrell says in her recollections, in *N. E. Hist. and Geneal. Reg.*, April, 1860, p. 150: "When the British troops came here they were lodged in a sugar-house in Brattle Square, which belonged to Mrs. Inman. I think there were three thousand of them. The officers lodged in the house of Madam Apthorp, in which I now live." But this paper is somewhat confused in other respects, if not in this. See John Adams's *Works*, ii. 213. — Ed.]

[2] [There is in the Charity Building collection a draft of a letter from the selectmen, Nov. 12, 1768, to Pownall and De Berdt, as endorsed by William Cooper, "on the present deplorable condition of this town, . . . changed from a free city to an almost garrison state." — Ed.]

[3] Lord North, eldest son of the Earl of Guilford, entered the cabinet at the age of thirty-five, and remained fifteen years, during the most crit-

ical period in English history. He was always a favorite of the king, and a recognized leader in the ministry. He never understood the charac-

ter or claims of the American people, and consequently favored a mistaken policy towards them, to which he adhered throughout the war.

[4] At the early age of forty-one. Bancroft, in summing up the character of Townshend, aptly calls him "the most celebrated statesman who has left nothing but errors to account for his fame," vi. 99.

Burke defended the Colonies, and denounced as illegal and unconstitutional the order requiring the General Court to rescind their resolutions. Barrington accused the Americans as traitors, adding, "The troops have been sent thither to bring rioters to justice." Lord North defended the recent act of Parliament, and said that he would never think of repealing it until he should see America " prostrate at his feet."

" Depend upon it," said Hillsborough to one of the colonial agents, " Parliament will not suffer their authority to be trampled upon. We wish to avoid severities towards you; but if you refuse obedience to our laws the whole fleet and army of England shall enforce it."

The indictment against the Colonies was presented in sixty papers laid before Parliament. Both Houses declared that the proceedings of the Massachusetts Assembly, in opposing the revenue acts, were unconstitutional; that the circular-letter tended to create unlawful combinations; and that the Boston convention was proof of a design of setting up an independent authority; and both Houses proposed, under the provisions of an obsolete act of Henry VIII., to transport to England " for trial and condign punishment," in direct violation of trial by jury, the chief authors and instigators of the late disorders. In the famous debate of this session, Burke, Barré, Pownall, and Dowdeswell spoke eloquently in behalf of the Colonies; but the address and resolutions were carried by a large majority.

After being nearly a year without a Legislature, Massachusetts was again permitted by the Governor, in the name of the King, to send its representatives to a General Court convened, according to the charter, on the last Wednesday in May, 1769. The first business was a protest against the breach of their privileges, and a petition to the Governor to have the troops removed from Boston, as it was inconsistent with the Assembly's dignity and freedom to deliberate in the presence of an armed force. They declined to enter upon the business of supplies, or anything else except the consideration of their grievances. The Governor refused to grant their petition, alleging want of authority over His Majesty's forces; and after vainly waiting a fortnight for them to vote him his year's salary, he adjourned the Assembly to Cambridge, and informed them that he was about to repair to England to lay the state of the province before His Majesty. The Assembly thereupon passed a unanimous vote, one hundred and nine members being present, to petition the king " to remove Sir Francis Bernard[1] forever from this government."[2] It has always been believed that much of the difficulty between Massachusetts and Great Britain was owing to the total unfitness of Bernard for the important position which he held during nine eventful years. His frequent misrepresentations of the spirit and conduct of the colonists are a matter of record. He left no friends behind him. Indeed his departure was an occasion of public rejoicing. " The bells were rung, guns

---

[1] Bernard had recently received a baronetcy, "a most ill-timed favor, when he had so grievously failed in gaining the affections or the confidence of any order or rank of men within his province." Mahon, *History of England*, v. 241.

[2] *Journal*, House of Representatives, 1769, 36.

were fired from Mr. Hancock's wharf, Liberty Tree was covered with flags, and in the evening a great bonfire was made upon Fort Hill."[1]

Lieut.-Governor Hutchinson succeeded to the chair as chief magistrate. He was a native of Boston, was acquainted with public affairs, and for many years had held more important offices than any other man in the province; but his career had been so often marred by duplicity and avarice that very little hope was cherished of any improvement in the administration. His failure was in part owing to the difficulty he found in trying to serve both England and America, with a decided preference in favor of the former, at a time when the opinions and interests of the two countries were rapidly becoming distinct. He was not the man for the times.[2] When the Massachusetts Assembly, sitting at Cambridge, had refused to grant the supplies demanded by Bernard, that functionary prorogued it to the tenth of January. When that date arrived, Hutchinson, under arbitrary instructions from Hillsborough, prorogued it still further to the middle of March.

Meanwhile the non-importation agreements had become so general as to produce a visible effect upon British commerce. Exports from England to America had fallen off seriously, and English merchants were really injured more than the Americans by the narrow revenue policy of the Government. Lord North, perceiving this, caused a circular-letter to be sent to the Colonies, proposing to favor the removal of duties from all articles, except tea, enumerated in the late act. This was evidently a measure of expediency, dictated wholly by self-interest; and as by retaining the duty on tea there was no surrender of the obnoxious claim contained in the declaratory act, it did not materially affect the situation in America.

Boston at this time, in a legal town-meeting,[3] issued an *Appeal to the World*, prepared by Samuel Adams, vindicating itself from the aspersions of Bernard, Gage, Hood, and the revenue officers. The Appeal says: —

"We should yet be glad that the ancient and happy union between Great Britain and this country might be restored. The taking off the duties on paper, glass, and

---

[1] Hutchinson, iii. 254. [See Dr. Ellis's estimate of Bernard in Vol. II. of this History, p. 65. The Governor left his estate on Jamaica Pond, July 31, 1769, and embarked the next day from the Castle. Lady Bernard did not leave the estate till December, 1770. — ED.]

[2] Hutchinson's *History of Massachusetts Bay* deserves honorable mention as a work of rare ability and candor, for which students of our history will always be grateful. [See Dr. Ellis's estimate of Hutchinson's administration in Vol. II. p 69; and that by Frothingham in his *Warren*, p. 107. — ED.]

[3] [Cooper, the town clerk, issued the warrant for this meeting, Sept. 28, 1761, and the meeting was held, October 4. A contemporary account (in the Chalmers papers, ii. 37, in the *Sparks MSS.* in Harvard College Library) says that Cooper read the letters to the meeting, "and took a good deal of pains to make the Governor appear as ridiculous as possible, which generally occasioned a grin of applause." Not long before this, the Sons of Liberty had dined together, Aug. 14, 1769, at Dorchester, and there is a list of their names in *Mass. Hist. Soc. Proc.*, August, 1869. John Adams's *Works*, ii. 218.

William Cooper, who figures largely in the town's transactions at this time, was a son of the Rev. William Cooper, D.D., of the Brattle Street Church: was born Oct. 1, 1721, and died Nov. 28, 1809. He was first chosen town clerk in 1761, and held the office till his death. In 1755-56 he was a representative to the General Court. From 1759 to 1800 he was Register of Probate. He is buried in the Granary Burial-ground. He lived on Hanover Street. He married, April 26, 1745, Katharine, daughter of Jacob Wendell, and had sixteen children. See notices in *Boston Patriot*, Dec. 6, 1809, and *Evening Transcript*, July 7, 1881. — ED.]

painters' colors, upon commercial principles only, will not give satisfaction. Discontent runs through the continent upon much higher principles. Our rights are invaded by the revenue acts; therefore, until they are all repealed, . . . and the troops recalled, . . . the cause of our just complaints cannot be removed."

29th December 1769

SIGNATURES OF THE TOWN'S COMMITTEE.[1]

Society in Boston was thoroughly moved by the prevailing sentiment.[2] Three hundred wives subscribed to a league agreeing not to drink any tea

[1] [These autographs are from a letter sent by the town to Dennis De Berdt, the colony's agent in England, in order that through him "our friends in Parliament may be acquainted with the difficulties the trade labors by means of those acts." It recapitulates how the merchants and traders of Boston had entered into an agreement, August, 1768, not to import goods from Great Britain after Jan. 1, 1770, and had made a further agreement, Oct. 17, 1769, that no goods should be sent from here till the revenue acts be repealed; and how the other colonies had not gone to the same extent; and so they informed De Berdt that they had notified their correspondents to ship goods with the express condition that the act imposing duties on tea, glass, paper, and colors be totally repealed, and had forwarded to him papers with their views on the matter. The original is in a collection of a part of the papers of Arthur Lee, who succeeded De Berdt as the agent of Massachusetts, and thus retained many of the documents emanating from the province and from Boston during the early days of the controversy. The younger Richard Henry Lee, after writing the Lives of the elder of his name and of Arthur Lee, divided the manuscripts which had come to him among three institutions, — the Libraries of Harvard College, of the University of Virginia, and of the American Philosophical Society in Philadelphia. No recognizable principle of adaptation was followed in the division, sets being broken, — those now in Virginia containing many papers of the utmost interest for Boston history, and in some cases when others closely allied with them are in the Harvard College collection. The Editor has been kindly entrusted with these other collections by their respective guardians. Those in the College Library have been calendared in print under his direction. — Eds.]

[2] [Richard Frothingham has minutely traced the progress of events and feelings of the people during this period. — from October, 1768, to the Massacre, — in his papers, "The Sam Adams

until the revenue act should be repealed. The young, unmarried women followed their example, and signed a document beginning as follows : " We, the daughters of those Patriots who have appeared . . . for the public interest, . . . do now with pleasure engage with them in denying ourselves the drinking of foreign tea."[1] . . . Even the children caught the spirit of patriotism, and imitated their elders in maintaining what they considered to be their " constitutional " rights.[2]

It was now nearly a year and a half since the troops had come to Boston, and their presence was a continual source of irritation to the inhabitants. Their services were not wanted ; their parades were offensive ; their bearing often insulting. Quarrels would occasionally arise between individual soldiers and citizens. " The troops greatly corrupt our morals," said Dr. Cooper, " and are in every sense an oppression. May Heaven soon deliver us from this great evil !"[3]

In this state of things, any unusual excitement might at any time occasion disastrous results. Towards the end of February an event occurred which threw the public mind into a ferment, and prepared the way for the tragic scenes of the fifth of March. A few of the merchants had rendered themselves unpopular by continuing to sell articles which had been proscribed. One of them in particular[4] had incurred such displeasure that his store was marked by the crowd with a wooden image as one to be shunned. One of his friends, a well known informer,[5] attempted to remove the image, but was driven back by the mob. Greatly exasperated, he fired a random shot among them and mortally wounded a young lad,[6] who died the following evening. The funeral was attended by five hundred children, walking in front of the bier ; six of his school-mates held the pall, followed by thirteen hundred of the inhabitants. The bells of the town were tolled, and the whole community partook of the feeling of sadness and indignation that innocent blood had been shed in the streets of Boston.[7]

A few days later, a still more serious occurrence took place. On Friday, March 2, two soldiers, belonging to the Twenty-ninth Regiment, were passing Gray's rope-walk, near the present Pearl Street, and got into a quarrel with one of the workmen. Insults and threats were freely exchanged, and the soldiers then went off and found some of their comrades, who returned with them and challenged the ropemakers to a boxing-match. A fight

Regiments," in *Atlantic Monthly*, June, August, 1862, and November, 1863 ; matter which is only epitomized in his *Life of Warren*. John Mein, the printer, had refused to join in any non-importation agreement, and his name had been publicly proclaimed as one to be avoided in trade. He in turn printed the *State of the Importation of Great Britain with the Port of Boston from January to August*, 1768, and showed some of his detractors in the light of importers. See Henry Stevens's *Historical Collections*, i. No. 393. — Ed.]

[1] *Boston Gazette*, Feb. 12, 1770, *et seq.* ; Lossing, *Field-Book*, i. 488.

[2] Lossing, " 1776," p. 90.

[3] Rev. S. Cooper to Governor Thomas Pownall, Jan. 1, 1770.

[4] Theophilus Lillie.

[5] Ebenezer Richardson, who lived near by.

[6] Christopher Snider.

[7] *Evening Post*, Feb. 26, 1770. [See Hutchinson ; Gordon, i. 276 ; John Adams's *Works*, ii. 227. — Ed.]

ensued, in which sticks and cutlasses were freely used. Several were
wounded on both sides, but none were killed. The proprietor and others
interposed, and prevented further disturbance.[1] The next day it was reported that the fight would be resumed on Monday. Colonel Carr, commander of the Twenty-ninth, complained to the Governor of the conduct of
the rope-makers. Hutchinson laid the matter before the council, some of
whom freely expressed the opinion that the only way to prevent such colli-
sions was to withdraw the troops to the Castle; but no precautionary measures were taken. At an early hour on Monday evening, March 5, numerous
parties of men and boys were strolling through the streets, and whenever
they met any of the soldiers a sharp altercation took place. The ground
was frozen and covered with a slight fall of snow, and a young moon shed
its mild light upon the scene. Small bands of soldiers were seen passing
between the main guard[2] and Murray's barracks in Brattle Street, armed
with clubs and cutlasses. They were met by a crowd of citizens carrying
canes and sticks. Taunts and insults soon led to blows. Some of the
soldiers levelled their firelocks, and threatened to "make a lane" through
the crowd. Just then an officer[3] on his way to the barracks, finding the
passage obstructed by the affray, ordered the men into the yard and had
the gate shut. The alarm-bell, however, had called out the people from
their homes, and many came down towards King Street, supposing there
was a fire there. When the occasion of the disturbance was known, the
well disposed among them advised the crowd to return home; but others
shouted: "To the main guard! To the main guard! That's the nest!"
Upon this they moved off towards King Street, some going up Cornhill,
some through Wilson's Lane, and others through Royal Exchange Lane.
Shortly after nine o'clock an excited party approached the Custom House,
which stood on the north side of King Street, at the lower corner of
Exchange Lane, where a sentinel was standing at his post. "There's the
soldier who knocked me down!" said a boy whom the sentinel, a few minutes before, had hit with the but-end of his musket. "Kill him! Knock
him down!" cried several voices. The sentinel retreated up the steps and
loaded his gun. "The lobster is going to fire," exclaimed a boy who stood
by. "If you fire you must die for it," said Henry Knox,[4] who was passing.

[1] [See Drake, *Landmarks*, 274 It was men
of the Fourteenth Regiment who were engaged
in this affair, and their barracks were in the
modern Atkinson Street. — Ed.]
[2] The "main guard" was located at the head
of King Street, directly opposite the south door
of the Town House The soldiers detailed for
daily guard-duty met here for assignment to
their several posts.
[3] Captain Goldfinch.
[4] Afterward general, and secretary of war.
[Knox was of Scotch-Presbyterian stock from the
north of Ireland, and his family belonged to the
parish of Moorhead, the pastor of the Long Lane

meeting-house. His father, William, a ship-
master, had married Mary, a daughter of Robert
Campbell; and Henry was their seventh son,
and was born in 1750, in a house which Drake,
*Life of Henry Knox*, p. 9, depicts, and says was
standing, in 1873, on Sea Street, opposite the
head of Drake's wharf. Losing his father in
1762, Henry went into the employ of Wharton &
Bowes, who had succeeded the year before to
the stand of Daniel Henchman, on the south
corner of State and Washington streets. Knox
was in this employ when the massacre occurred;
but the next year (1771) he started business on
his own account on the same street, about where

"I don't care," replied the sentry; "if they touch me, I'll fire." While he was saying this, snowballs and other missiles were thrown at him, whereupon he levelled his gun, warned the crowd to keep off, and then shouted to the main guard across the street, at the top of his voice, for help. A sergeant, with a file of seven men, was sent over at once, through the crowd, to protect him. The sentinel then came down the steps and fell in with the file, when the order was given to prime and load. Captain Thomas Preston of the Twenty-ninth soon joined his men, making the whole number in arms ten.[1] About fifty or sixty people had now gathered before the Custom House. When they saw the soldiers loading, some of them stepped forward, shouting, whistling, and daring them to fire. "You are cowardly rascals," they said; "lay aside your guns and we are ready for you." "Are the soldiers loaded?" inquired a bystander. "Yes," answered the Captain, "with powder and ball." "Are they going to fire on the inhabitants?" asked another. "They cannot," said the Captain, "without my orders." "For God's sake," said Knox, seizing Preston by the coat, "take your men back again. If they fire, your life must answer for the consequences." "I know what I'm about," said he, hastily; and then, seeing his men pressing the people with their bayonets, while clubs were being freely used, he rushed in among them. The confusion was now so great, some calling out, "Fire, fire if you dare!" and others, "Why don't you fire?" that no one could tell whether Captain Preston ordered the men to fire or not; but with or without orders, and certainly without any legal warning, seven of the soldiers, one after another, fired upon the citizens, three of whom were killed outright: Crispus Attucks,[2] Samuel Gray, and James Caldwell; and two others, Samuel Maverick[3] and Patrick Carr, died soon after from their wounds. Six others were badly wounded. It is not known that any of the eleven took part in the disturbance except Attucks, who had been a conspicuous leader of the mob.

When the firing began the people instinctively fell back, but soon after returned for the killed and wounded. Captain Preston restrained his

the *Globe* newspaper now is, calling his establishment the "London Bookstore." At least one book, *Catalogue on the Gout*, bears his imprint, 1772, and at the end of it is a list of medical and other books which he had imported. *Brodey Catalogue*, No. 1585. See H. G. Otis's letter in *N. E. Hist. and Geneal. Reg.*, July, 1876, p. 362. In November, 1774, Knox writes to Long-

man in London: "The magazines and new publications concerning the American dispute are the only things which I desire you to send at present." It will be remembered that Knox but six months before this had married a daughter

of the royalist secretary of the province, Thomas Flucker, who had vainly tried to prevent the union; and a year from the day of their marriage Knox had shipped out of Boston clandestinely, to avoid interception by Gage, while his wife concealed in her quilted skirts the sword her husband was afterwards to make honorable.— ED.]

[1] Some accounts say eight.

[2] Usually called a mulatto, sometimes a slave; and in the *American Historical Record* for December, 1872, he is held to have been a half-breed Indian. [George Livermore gives us a glimpse of the past life of Crispus Attucks as a slave, in his "Historical Research on Negroes as Slaves," in *Mass. Hist. Soc. Proc.* 1862, Aug., p. 173. See also *N. E. Hist. and Geneal. Reg.*, Oct. 1859, p. 300.— ED.]

[3] [See Sumner's *East Boston*, p. 171.— ED.]

men from a second discharge, and ordered them back to the main guard.
The drums beat to arms, and several companies of the Twenty-ninth formed,
under Colonel Carr, in three divisions, in the neighborhood of the Town
House. And now the alarm was everywhere given. The church bells
were rung, the town drums beat to arms, and King Street was soon thronged
with citizens who poured in from all directions. The sight of the mangled
bodies of the slain sent terror and indignation through their ranks. The
excitement surpassed anything which Boston had ever known before. It was
indeed a "night of consternation." No one knew what would happen next;
but in that awful hour the people were guided by wise and prudent leaders,
who restrained their passions and turned to the law for justice. About ten
o'clock the Lieut.-Governor appeared on the scene and called for Captain
Preston, to whom he put some sharp and searching questions. Forced
by the crowd he then went to the Town House, and soon appeared on the
balcony, where he spoke with much feeling and power concerning the
unhappy event, and promised to order an inquiry in the morning, saying
"the law should have its course; he would live and die by the law." On
being informed that the people would not disperse until Captain Preston
was arrested, he at once ordered a court of inquiry; and after consultation
with the military officers, he succeeded in having the troops removed to
their barracks, after which the people began to disperse. Preston's examination lasted three hours, and resulted in his being bound over for trial.
The soldiers were also placed under arrest. It was three o'clock in the
morning before Hutchinson retired to his house. By his judicious exertions he succeeded in calming a tumult which, had it been left to itself,
might in a single night have involved the town in a conflict of much greater
proportions. Early in the morning, large numbers of people from the surrounding country flocked into the town to learn the details of the tragedy,
and to confer with the citizens as to what was to be done. Faneuil Hall
was thrown open for an informal meeting at eleven o'clock. The town
clerk, William Cooper, acted as chairman until the selectmen could be
summoned from the council chamber, where they were in conference with
the Lieut.-Governor. On their appearance, Thomas Cushing was chosen
moderator; and Dr. Cooper, brother of the town clerk, opened the meeting with prayer. Several witnesses brought in testimony concerning the
events of the previous night. A committee of fifteen, including Adams,
Cushing, Hancock, and Molineux, was chosen to wait on the Lieut.-Gov-
ernor and inform him that the inhabitants and soldiery could no longer live
together in safety; and that nothing could restore peace and prevent further carnage but the immediate removal of the troops.[1] In the afternoon
at three o'clock a regular town-meeting was convened at the same place, by
legal warrant, to consider what measures could be taken to preserve the

[1] [Dr. Belknap records an anecdote told by him and demanded the removal of the troops
Governor Hancock, of the trepidation which after the massacre. *Mass. Hist. Soc. Proc.*, March,
seized Hutchinson when the committee went to 1858, p. 368. — I.D.]

June 29 1771.

In the name & by order of
the House of Representatives

I am with respect
your most humble serv[t]

Thomas Cushing Speaker

[This cut follows a painting which has for   and is believed, from the costume, to represent
many years hung in the Essex Institute, Salem,   the Patriot of that name; though the earlier

SAMUEL ADAMS.[1]

peace of the town. The attendance was so large that the meeting was adjourned to the Old South, which was soon crowded to its utmost capacity.

Speaker of the same name, who died in 1748, may possibly have been the sitter. The painting itself has no inscription, as the courteous Librarian, Dr. Henry Wheatland, informs me. In 1876 a descendant caused a copy of it to be made for Independence Hall, Philadelphia, in the belief that it represented the later Thomas Cushing. He was born in Bromfield Street, on the spot long occupied by the public house of that name. — ED.]

[1] [This cut follows the larger of Copley's portraits of Adams, and was painted when he was forty-nine. The smaller and later one has already been given in Vol. II. p. 438. The present picture for many years hung in Faneuil Hall, and is now in the Art Museum; it has been engraved before in Wells's *Life of Samuel Adams*, vol. i., in Bancroft's *United States*, vol. vii., and elsewhere. It represents the Patriot, clad in dark red, defending the rights of the people under the

Samuel Adams presented the report of the committee, which was that they could not obtain a promise of the removal of more than one of the regiments at present. " Both regiments or none ! " was the cry with which the meeting received this announcement. The answer was voted to be unsatisfactory; and another committee was appointed, consisting of Samuel Adams, John Hancock, William Molineux, William Phillips, Joseph Warren, Joshua Henshaw, and Samuel Pemberton, to inform the Lieut.-Governor that nothing less than the total and immediate removal of the troops would satisfy the people. At a late hour the committee returned with a favorable report, which was received by the meeting with expressions of the greatest satisfaction. Before adjourning, a strong military watch was provided for; and the whole subject of the public defence was left in the hands of a "committee of safety," consisting of those who had just waited on the Lieut.-Governor.

On Thursday, March 8, the funeral of the slain was an occasion of mournful interest to the whole community. The stores were generally closed. The bells of Boston, Charlestown, Cambridge, and Roxbury were tolled. Never before, it was said, was there so large an assemblage in the streets of Boston. The procession started from the scene of the massacre in King Street, and proceeded through the main street six deep, followed by a long train of carriages, to the Middle or Granary Burying-ground, where the bodies of the victims were deposited in one grave.

After the removal of the troops to the Castle, nothing occurred to disturb the usual quiet of the town. The people waited patiently for the law to have its course. In October, Preston's case came on for trial in the Superior Court, followed in November by that of the soldiers implicated in the massacre. Through the exertions of Samuel Adams and others, the best legal talent in the province was secured on both sides. The prosecution was conducted by Robert Treat Paine, in the absence of the king's attorney.[1] Auchmuty, the prisoners' counsel, had the valuable assistance of John Adams and Josiah Quincy, the distinguished Patriots, who generously consented to take the position, — a severe ordeal at such a time, — in order that the town might be free from any charge of unfairness, and that the accused might have the advantage of every legal indulgence.[2] As a

Charter, — as he may be supposed to have appeared when he confronted Hutchinson and his council on the day after the massacre. Wells, *Life of Adams,* i. 475. The Copley head of Sam Adams was engraved by J. Norman in *An Impartial History of the War in America,* Boston, 1781. The journals of the Boston committee of correspondence, as well as the papers of Sam Adams, are in the possession of Bancroft the historian. Frothingham, *Life of Warren,* p. vii. Wells, *Life of Sam Adams,* vol. i. pp. vi. and x., gives a particular account of the Adams papers. Bancroft's *United States,* p. vi. preface. See an estimate of Adams in Mr. Goddard's ch. — Ed.]

[1] [This was Jonathan Sewall, who, as John Adams says, "disappeared." It is probable that Samuel Quincy — a few months later to be made solicitor-general — assisted Paine, as stated by Ward in his edition of *Curwen's Journal,* and by Mr. Morse in Vol. IV.; though I find no contemporary authority for such statement, unless what John Adams says (*Works,* x. 201) in connection with the soldiers' trial applies as well to Preston's. Quincy is known, however, to have been on the Government side in the soldiers' trials. — Ed.]

[2] [See the chapter on "The Bench and Bar," by John T. Morse, Jr., in Vol. IV. — Ed.]

*Josiah, Quincy jun'.*[1]

result of the trial, Preston was acquitted; six of the soldiers were brought in "not guilty;" and two were found guilty of manslaughter, branded in the

[1] [Of this picture there is this account by Miss E. S. Quincy in Mason's *Life of Gilbert Stuart*, p. 244: "There was an engraving that his widow, Mrs. Abigail Quincy, considered an excellent likeness. This print, Stuart had declined to copy; but after reading the memoir of J. Quincy, Jr., published in 1825, he said: 'I must paint the portrait of that man;' and requested that the print, and the portrait of his brother Samuel Quincy, by Copley, should be sent to his studio." Miss Quincy says in a private letter: "The portrait was entirely satisfactory to my father and Mrs. Storer. The cast in his eye was one of his characteristics which they would not have allowed to be omitted." Jonathan Mason, who studied law in Mr. Quincy's office, Mr. Gardiner Greene, who saw him in London, Dr. Holbrook, of Milton, and many others testified to the likeness. There is an estimate of Quincy in Mr. Goddard's chapter in this volume. Quincy lived on the present Washington Street, a little south of Milk Street.

hand in open court, and then discharged. These trials must ever be regarded as a signal instance of that desire for impartial justice which characterized the American people throughout the stormy period which ushered in the Revolution.[1]

The manuscript of instructions to the representatives of the town, in his handwriting (1770), is noted in *Mass. Hist. Soc. Proc.*, December, 1873, p. 216. See also Frothingham's *Warren*, p. 156. His family relations can be traced in Vol. II. p. 547, and in the accounts of the Bromfield and Phillips family in the same volume pp. 543, 548. His father-in-law was William Phillips, who was the son of the Rev. Samuel Phillips of Andover, and who coming to Boston entered into business connections with Edward Bromfield, a rich merchant, whose daughter he afterward married, in 1764, and whose house on Beacon Street, figured in Vol. II. p. 521, he bought and lived in till his death in 1804. He amassed a large fortune, which has been transmitted to our day, though now mainly possessed by a collateral branch of the family. He took the Patriot side in the Revolution; and in August, 1774, Josiah Quincy, Jr., writes to Samuel Adams, then in Philadelphia: "It is very difficult to keep our poor in order. Mr. Phillips has done wonders among them. I do not know what we should do without him." After his daughter (Mrs. Quincy) lost her husband in 1775, she with her young son, the future President Quincy, lived with her father till 1786. Mr. Phillips's two younger daughters — twins, born in 1756, Sarah and Hannah — married respectively Edward Dowse and Major Samuel Shaw, who had been an aid to General Knox

*Samuel Shaw*

in the Revolution. Both were pioneers in opening trade with China after the war, and Shaw's memoir has been written by President Quincy. Shaw lived in Bulfinch Place, in a house built for him in 1793 by Charles Bulfinch; and it is to-day, shorn of its ample grounds, known as Hotel Waterston. An account of Phillips can be found in the *American Quarterly Register*, xiii., No. 1. — Ed.]

[1] For details see *Lives of John Adams and Josiah Quincy*. The brief used by the former is in the Boston Public Library. [It is a small brochure of ten leaves, six by four inches, fastened by a pin, and four of the leaves are blank. The annexed *facsimile* is of the opening paragraph. Kidder, who formerly owned the document, has printed it in his *Boston Massacre*, p. 10.

*Evidence of Commotions that Evening.*
*Saml Crawford went home ½ past 8 o'clock — met Numbers of People going down towards ye Town House with Sticks — a Goldsmith saw above a dozen with Sticks, in Quaker Lane and Quernlane met many going towards the old — very great Sticks, pretty large Cudgels, not coming walking barrel*

Sampson Salter Blowers, who assisted Adams and Quincy, had graduated at Harvard in 1763,

*Sampr S Blowers*

and was only made a barrister in 1773: and in the next year married a daughter of Benjamin Kent, with whom he went to Nova Scotia at the time of the loyalist exodus. The presiding judge was the younger Lynde, whose portrait is

*Benjn Lynde*

given in Vol. II. p. 558. All that remains of his charge is given in the appendix of *The Diaries of Benjamin Lynde, and of Benjamin Lynde, Jr.*, Boston, privately printed, 1880.

John Adams wrote to J. Morse in 1816 (*Works of John Adams*, x. 201) that the report of Preston's trial "was taken down, and transmitted to England, by a Scottish or English stenographer, without any known authority but his own. The British Government have never permitted it to see the light, and probably never will." When the trial of William Wemms and seven other soldiers came on, Nov. 27, 1770, the same short-hand writer, John Hodgson, was employed; and the published report, — entitled *The Trial of William Wemms, . . . for the Murder of Crispus Attucks. . . . Published by permission of the Court. . . . Boston: printed by J. Fleeming, and sold at his Printing Office, nearly opposite the White Horse Tavern in Newbury Street. M.DCC.LXX.* — makes a duodecimo of two hundred and seventeen pages. It gives the evidence and pleas of counsel. The last seven pages are occupied with a report, "from the minutes of a gentleman who attended," of the trial, December 12, of Edward Manwaring and

Previous to 1770 the people of Boston had celebrated the Gunpowder Plot annually with public demonstrations. After the Boston massacre, the

others, who were accused by several persons of firing on the crowd during the massacre from an adjacent window in the Custom House; but they were easily acquitted. This little volume was reprinted in Boston in 1807 and 1824, and again in Kidder's monograph in 1870. The plan of King Street, used at the trials, prepared by Paul Revere, is in the collection of Judge Mellen Chamberlain, of the Boston Public Library. An examination of the reports of the trial is made in P. W. Chandler's *American Criminal Trials*, i.

A minute narrative of the events was printed between black lines in the *Boston Gazette* of March 12, but the papers of the day made few references to the event till after the trial, when more or less discontent with the verdict was manifested. Such particularly marked a series of articles in the *Gazette*, signed "Vindex" (Sam Adams), which reflected upon the arguments of the counsel for defence. Buckingham, *Reminiscences*, i. 168.

Some verses inscribed upon one of the pictures of the massacre closed as follows, referring to Boston and Preston : —

"Should venal courts, the scandal of the land,
Snatch the relentless villain from her hand,
Keen execrations, on this plate inscribed,
Shall reach a judge who never can be bribed."

A letter from William Palfrey to John Wilkes, dated Boston, March 13 (1770), is printed in *Mass. Hist. Soc. Proc.*, March, 1863, p. 480. (See also Sparks, *American Biography*, new series, vol. viii.) And on p. 484 is printed one from Thomas Hutchinson to Lord Hillsborough on the same theme.

There are some particulars entered upon the Town Records of the statements made at the meeting at Faneuil Hall the next forenoon ; but so many were ready to testify, that a committee was appointed to gather the evidence. The annexed autographs are attached to a letter addressed to the agent of Massachusetts in London, the original of which is in the Lee collection of papers in the University of Virginia Library ; and with the letter was sent a copy of a *Narrative* authorized by the town. A similar letter, and other copies, were sent to various important people in England, — a list of whom, together with the letter, is printed at the end of some copies of the *Narrative*, which was also probably

drawn up by the same gentlemen, and, as printed, is called *A short Narrative of the Horrid*

*Boston New England march 28: 1770*

*James Bowdoin*

*Sam'l Pemberton,*

*Joseph Warren*

*Massacre in Boston perpetrated in the evening of the Fifth Day of March, 1770, by Soldiers of the XXIXth Regiment, with some Observations on the State of Things prior to that Catastrophe. Boston : printed by order of the Town, by Messrs. Edes & Gill.* MDCCLXX. It had an appendix of depositions, including one of Jeremiah Belknap ; but another, of Joseph Belknap, is contained in the *Belknap Papers*, i. 69, in the cabinet of the Massachusetts Historical Society. A large folding plate showed the scene in State Street. It was immediately reprinted in London, in at least three editions, — two by W. Bingley, in Newgate Street, with the large folding plate re-engraved ; and the third by E. and C. Dilby, with a smaller plate, a *fac-simile* of which, somewhat reduced, is given on the next page. The supplement of the *Boston Evening Post*, June 18, 1770, has news from London, May 5, announcing the republication of it, and stating that the frontispiece was engraved from a copper-plate print sent over with the "authenticated narrative."

Copies of this *Short Narrative* were sent at once to England, but the remainder of the edition was not published, for fear of giving "an undue bias to the minds of the jury," till after the trial, when *Additional Observations*, of twelve pages, were added to it. These were likewise published separately. Both of these documents were reprinted in New York in 1849, and again at Albany in 1870, in Mr. Kidder's *History of the Boston Massacre*. In this supplemental publication it was intimated that the friends of Government had sent despatches "home " "to represent the town in a disadvantageous light." It is certain that a tract did appear shortly in London, called : *A fair Account of the late*

fifth of March was observed until the peace of 1783,[1] when the Fourth of
July celebration was substituted by the town authorities. Unquestionably
the influence of the Boston massacre upon the growing sentiment of independence throughout the colonies was very great.[2] Public opinion was
immediately shaped by it, and the remaining ties binding America to
Britain were everywhere visibly relaxed. "On that night," wrote John

*The Massacre perpetrated in King Street Boston on March 5th 1770, in which
Messrs. Sam'l Gray, Sam'l Maverick James Caldwell Crispus Attucks
Patrick Carr were Killed, six others Wounded two of them Mortally*

*unhappy Disturbance at Boston in New England;
extracted from the Depositions that have been
made concerning it by persons of all parties: with
an Appendix containing some affidavits and other
evidence relating to this affair, not mentioned in
the Narrative of it that has been published at Boston. London: printed for B. White, in Fleet
Lane; MDCCLXX.* There is a copy in Harvard
College Library. It is the Government view of
the massacre, and is duly fortified by counter
depositions, chiefly by officers and men of the
garrison. Hutchinson has given his account of
it in his posthumous third volume, and Gordon
in his first volume. Stedman's account in his
*American War* is also at variance with the
town's narrative.

Of the later historians Mr. Frothingham in
the last of his papers on "The Sam Adams
Regiments" (*Atlantic Monthly,* November, 1863),
and in his *Life of Warren,* ch. vi., has given a
very excellent account, "carefully collating the
evidence that appears to be
authentic;" but he confesses
it is vain to reconcile all statements. The events are also
minutely described in Wells's
*Life of Samuel Adams,* i. 308.
Bancroft, *United States,* vol.
vi. ch. xliii., examines the evidence for provocation, and
concludes Preston ordered
the firing. He cites, through
the chapter, his authorities.
— ED.]

[1] Orations were delivered
on the successive anniversa-
ries by Thomas Young, Joseph
Warren, Benjamin Church,
John Hancock, Joseph War-
ren, Peter Thacher, Benjamin
Hichborn, Jonathan W. Aus-
tin, William Tudor, Jonathan
Mason, Thomas Dawes,
George R. Minot, and Thomas
Welsh. [These, having been
printed separately, were collected and issued by Peter
Edes in 1785, and reissued in
1807. There are accounts of
them and their authors in Loring's *Hundred Boston Orators.*
Paul Revere took the occasion
of the first anniversary of the
massacre, in 1771, to rouse the
sensibilities of the crowd by
giving illuminated pictures of
the event, with allegorical ac-
companiments, at the windows
of his house in North Square.
"The spectators," says the account in the
*Gazette,* "were struck with solemn silence, and
their countenances covered with a melancholy
gloom." — ED.]

[2] [See the letter to Franklin in *Mass. Hist. Soc.
Proc.,* November, 1865. Also Sparks's *Franklin,*
vii. 409. — ED.]

Adams long afterward, "the formation of American Independence was laid." "From that moment," said Mr. Webster on one occasion, "we may date the severance of the British empire."

On the very day of the Boston massacre Lord North brought in a bill to repeal the Townshend revenue act, with the exception of the preamble and the duty on tea, which were retained to signify the continued supremacy of Parliament. This proposal met with much opposition, but was finally carried, and approved by the king on April 12.

As the great principle at issue was not relinquished, this new measure of the Government gave but little satisfaction to the colonists. Trade, however, revived, and before the end of 1770 it was open in everything but tea.[1]

In the month of September Hutchinson received a royal order in effect introducing martial law into Massachusetts, in so far as to compel him to give up the fortress to General Gage, or such officer as he might appoint. This order was in direct contravention of the charter of the province, which gave the command of the militia and the forts to the civil Governor. After a little hesitation Hutchinson decided to obey the order, and, without consulting the council, he at once handed over the Castle to Colonel Dalrymple; and from that hour it remained in the possession of England until the evacuation of Boston in March, 1776. The Provincial Assembly, meeting at Cambridge for the third time, and keeping a day of fasting, humiliation, and prayer, entered a solemn protest against the new and insupportable grievances under which they labored.[2] At this time Franklin, Boston's honored son, was elected as the agent of Massachusetts to represent her cause before the king.[3] Certainly no better choice could have been made. In the fulness of his ripened powers, possessed of rare wisdom and integrity, and animated by a spirit of fervent patriotism, he discharged the grave duties of his position with conspicuous fidelity and zeal.

The next year was not marked by any very notable event. Hutchinson, who had now received his coveted commission as Governor, maintained a controversy with the Assembly upon several matters of legislation, and

[1] The self-imposed restrictions adopted by the colonists in reference to foreign articles had produced a great effect in checking extravagance, promoting domestic industry and economy, and opening to the people new sources of wealth. Home-made articles, which at first came into use from necessity, soon became fashionable. At Harvard College the graduating class of 1770 took their degrees in homespun.

[2] [John Adams was now a representative from Boston, succeeding Bowdoin, who had gone into the Council. See *John Adams's Works*, ii. 233. "Although Sam Adams was now the master-mover, John Adams seems to have succeeded to the post of legal adviser, which had been filled by Oxenbridge Thacher and James Otis." The four "Boston seats" were thus filled by Cushing (the Speaker), Hancock, Sam Adams, and John Adams; and to show their influence the journals indicate that three, and sometimes all of them, were on every important committee for a session which was much concerned with political movements. John Adams was at this period a resident of Boston from April, 1768, to April, 1771; but he still retained his office in Boston after removing his family to Braintree; and again he established a home in Queen Street, opposite the Court House, in 1772. — Eds.]

[3] [The choice of Franklin was made Oct. 24, 1770; his appointment, signed by Thomas Cushing, speaker, is among the Lee Papers, University of Virginia. See Mr. Towle's chapter in Vol. II. — Eds.]

arbitrarily insisted upon their meeting in Cambridge, until the opposition to it, became so strong that he was obliged to consent to a removal to Boston.[1] The House soon after censured the Governor for accepting a salary from the king in violation of the charter; and the popular indignation was still further aroused when it became known that royal stipends were provided for the judges in the province. This led to a town-meeting (Oct. 28, 1772), at which an address to his Excellency was prepared, requesting information of the truth of the report. The Governor declined to make public any of his official advices. Another petition was drafted at an adjourned meeting, requesting the Governor to convene the Assembly on the day to which it stood prorogued (December 2); and at the same time the meeting expressed its horror of the reported judicial establishment, as contrary not only to the charter but to the fundamental principles of common law. This petition also was rejected in a reply which was read several times at an adjourned meeting and voted "not satisfactory." It was then resolved that the inhabitants of Boston "have ever had and ought to have a right to petition the king, or his representative, for a redress of such grievances as they feel, or for preventing of such as they have reason to apprehend; and to communicate their sentiments to other towns." Adams now stood up and made that celebrated motion, which gave visible shape to the American Revolution, and endowed it with life and strength. The record[2] says: —

"It was then moved by Mr. Samuel Adams that a committee of correspondence[3] be appointed, to consist of twenty-one persons, to state the rights of the colonists, and of this province in particular, as men and Christians, and as subjects; and to communicate and publish the same to the several towns, and to the world, as the sense of this town, with the infringements and violations thereof that have been or from time to time may be made."

The motion was carried by a nearly unanimous vote; but some of the leading men were not prepared to serve on the committee. It was seen that the labors would be arduous, prolonged, and gratuitous; and although they did not oppose, neither did they cordially support a measure which was really greater than they imagined. The committee, however, was well

[1] [The instructions of the town, May 25, 1772, to Cushing and the other representatives, are given in the Mass. Hist. Soc. Proc., January, 1871, p. 9. The House later prepared an address of remonstrance to the king against taxation without representation, and, July 14, 1772, it was despatched, signed by Cushing. An original is among the Lee Papers, in the University of Virginia. — Ed.]

[2] Boston Town Records, November, 1772.

[3] [John Adams said that Sam Adams "invented" the committee of correspondence. Frothingham, Life of Warren, p. 200. There has been some controversy about the origin of these committees; but Bancroft, who has their papers, avers positively that Gordon's opinion (i. 312) of the idea originating with James Warren of Plymouth is erroneous. Bancroft's United States, vi. 428. See further, Wells's Samuel Adams, i. 509, ii. 62; Frothingham's Rise of the Republic, pp. 284, 312, 327; Barry's Massachusetts, ii. 448, and other references in Winsor's Handbook, p. 20. The town's committee of correspondence must not be confounded with the Assembly's committee. See R. Frothingham in Mass. Hist. Soc. Proc., Dec. 16, 1873. See earlier in this chapter for Mayhew's suggestion. See also Hutchinson, iii. 361; and Gordon, i. 314. — Ed.]

LIEUT.-GOVERNOR ANDREW OLIVER.[1]

constructed, with Adams and Warren and other citizens of well known character and the highest patriotism. Otis, though broken in health, was named chairman, as a compliment for his former services.

[1] [This cut follows Copley's portrait of Andrew Oliver, owned by Dr. F. E. Oliver, by whose kind permission it is copied. Perkins's *Copley*, p. 92. For his family connections see Mr. Whitmore's chapter in Vol. II. p. 530, and his more extended genealogy of the Olivers in *N. E. Hist. and Geneal. Reg.*, April, 1865, p. 101. The two sons of Daniel Oliver (who died 1732, leaving a bequest to the town; see Vol.

*And Oliver*

II. p. 539) were Andrew Oliver, the Lieut.-Governor (who died 1774, and was father of Andrew,

judge and mandamus councillor), and Chief-Justice Peter Oliver. They had close family rela-

*Peter Oliver*

tions with Governor Hutchinson, for Andrew's second wife, Mary, was sister of Hutchinson's wife, the two being daughters of William Sanford; and Dr. Peter Oliver, son of the chief-justice, married Sarah, daughter of Governor Hutchinson. Andrew, the mandamus councillor, married a sister of the second Judge Lynde, who presided at the massacre trials. The family of the Lieut.-Governor, by his second wife, were refugees with their uncle, the chief justice. — ED.]

This committee of correspondence met the next day and chose William Cooper as clerk. By a unanimous vote they gave to each other the pledge of honor "not to divulge any part of the conversation at their meetings to any person whatsoever, excepting what the committee itself should make known."

*June 8. 1774*

*By Order of the Committee of Correspondence for Boston*

*William Cooper Clerk.*

The work to be done was divided between them. Adams was appointed to prepare a statement of the rights of the colonists; Warren of the several violations of those rights; and Church was to draft a letter to the other towns.

On November 20 the report was presented at a legal meeting in Faneuil Hall. The statement of rights and of grievances, and the letter to the towns, were masterly presentations of the cause, and carried conviction throughout the province. Plymouth, Marblehead, Roxbury, and Cambridge responded at once to the call; and it was not long before committees of correspondence were everywhere established. The other Colonies accepted the plan.[1] Virginia saw in it the prospect of union throughout the continent. So did South Carolina. "An American Congress," wrote Samuel Adams to Arthur Lee (April 9, 1773), "is no longer the fiction of a political enthusiast."[2]

In the spring of 1773 the East India Company, finding itself embarrassed from the excessive accumulation of teas in England, owing to the persistent refusal of American merchants to import them, applied to Parliament for assistance, and obtained an act empowering the Company to export teas to America without paying the ordinary duty in England. This would enable the Company to sell at such low rates that it was thought the colonists would purchase, even with the tax of threepence on the pound. Accordingly ships were laden with the article and despatched to Charleston, Philadelphia, New York, and Boston, and persons were selected in each of these ports to act as consignees, or "tea commissioners" as they were called.

---

[1] [The report of the committee of correspondence, made Nov. 20, 1772, was, by order of the town, printed by Edes & Gill, as *The Votes and Proceedings of the Freeholders and other Inhabitants*. Frothingham, *Warren*, p. 211, etc., has much to show the effect this meeting was having throughout the colonies. — Ed.]

[2] Secret letters, written by Governor Hutchinson and Lieut.-Governor Oliver to friends in England, favoring military intervention and otherwise injuring the cause of the colonists, were discovered about this time through the agency of Franklin, and forwarded to the Patriots in Boston. The result was a formal petition to the king for the removal of the odious functionaries. These letters were printed in Boston in 1773, and in London in 1774. *Mass. Hist. Soc. Proc.*, 1858. [See further on this matter, with a note on the authorities, Vol. II. p. 80. John Adams saw them as early as March 22, 1773. (*Works*, ii. 318.) The letters were first published in Boston, June 16, 1773. Thomas Newell's "diary" in *Proc.*, October, 1877, p. 339. — Ed.]

When this news became known, all America was in a flame. The people were not to be duped by any such appeal to their cupidity. They had taken their stand upon a principle, and not until that was recognized would they withdraw their opposition. It seemed strange that England had not discerned that fact long before.

Nowhere was the feeling more intense on the subject than in Boston. The consignees were prominent men and friends of the Governor.[1] On the night of November 1 they were each one summoned to appear on the following Wednesday noon, at Liberty Tree, to resign their commissions. Handbills were also posted over the town, inviting citizens to meet at the same place.[2] On the day appointed, the bells rang from eleven to twelve o'clock, and the town-crier summoned the people to meet at Liberty Tree, which was decorated with a large flag. About five hundred assembled, including many of the leading Patriots. As the consignees failed to appear, a committee was appointed to wait upon them and request their resignation; and, in case they refused, to present a resolve to them declaring them to be enemies of their country. The committee, accompanied by many of the people, repaired to Clarke's warehouse and had a brief parley with the consignees, who refused to resign their trust.

A legal town-meeting was now called for, and the selectmen issued a warrant for one to be held on the fifth.[3] It was largely attended, and Hancock[4] was chosen moderator. A series of eight resolves was adopted, similar to those which had been recently passed in Philadelphia, and extensively circulated through the press. The consignees were again, through a committee, asked to resign; and again they refused, and the meeting adjourned.

On the seventeenth a vessel arrived, announcing that the tea-ships were on the way to Boston and might be hourly expected. Another legal meeting was immediately notified for the next day, at which Hancock was again the moderator. Word was sent to the consignees that it was the desire of the town that they would give a final answer whether they would resign their appointment. The answer came that they could not comply with the re-

---

[1] Two of them were his sons, Elisha and Thomas; the others were Richard Clarke and sons, Benj. Faneuil, Jr., and Joshua Winslow.

[2] Draper's *Gazette* of November 3 contained the following: —

"*To the Freemen of this and the neighboring towns:*

"GENTLEMEN, — You are desired to meet at Liberty Tree this day at twelve o'clock at noon; then and there to hear the persons, to whom the tea shipped by the East India Company is consigned, make a public resignation of their office as consignees, upon oath; and also swear that they will reship any teas that may be consigned to them by said Company, by the first vessel sailing for London.

"Boston, Nov. 3, 1773.          O. C., *Secretary.*

"‡ ‡ Show us the man that dare take down this."

Several of these handbills are in possession of the Mass. Hist. Society.

[3] This warrant is now in the possession of Judge Mellen Chamberlain.

[4] [Revere's portrait of Hancock is given in the text. It appeared in the *Royal Amer. Mag.*, March, 1774, which contains also Hancock's massacre oration of that year. On Nov. 11, 1773, Hutchinson had directed Hancock, as colonel of the cadets, to hold them in readiness for service. Frothingham, *Life of Warren*, p. 246, mentions the original of this order as being in the hands of the late Col. J. W. Sever. A curious engraving of "His Ex'y John Hancock, late President of the American Congress, J. Norman, sc.," appeared in *An Impartial History of the War in America*, Boston, 1781, vol. i. On the Hancock papers (most of which are printed in the *American Archives*) see *Massachusetts Historical Society Proceedings*, January, 1858, p. 271 and December, 1857; and Vol. IV. of this History, p. 5, *note*. — ED.]

quest.[1] Upon this the meeting dissolved, without passing any vote or expressing any opinion. "This sudden dissolution," says Hutchinson,[2] "struck more terror into the consignees than the most minatory resolves."

The whole matter was now understood to be in the hands of the committee of correspondence, who constituted the virtual government of the province.

On Sunday, November 28, the ship "Dartmouth," Captain Hall, after a sixty days' passage, appeared in the harbor, with one hundred and four-

The Hon.ble JOHN HANCOCK, Efq

teen chests of tea.[3] There was no time to be lost. Sunday though it was, the selectmen and the committee of correspondence held meetings to take immediate action against the entry of the tea. The consignees had gone to the Castle; but a promise was obtained from Francis Rotch, the owner of the vessel, that it should not be entered until Tuesday. The towns around Boston[4] were then invited to attend a mass meeting in Faneuil Hall the next morning.[5] Thousands were ready to respond to

---

[1] The answer is given in Frothingham's *Life of Warren*, p. 251.

[2] *History*, iii. 426.

[3] [The next morning, twenty-ninth, the vessel came up and anchored off Long Wharf (*Massachusetts Gazette*, November 29). The journal of the "Dartmouth" is in *Traits of the Tea-Party*, p. 230. — ED.]

[4] Dorchester, Roxbury, Brookline, Cambridge, and Charlestown.

[5] The following placard appeared on Monday morning:—

"FRIENDS! BRETHREN! COUNTRYMEN!

"That worst of plagues, the detested Tea, shipped for this port by the East India Company, is now arrived in this harbor. The hour of destruction, or manly opposition to

this summons, and the meeting was obliged to adjourn to the Old South. Boston, it was said, had never seen so large a gathering.[1] It was unanimously resolved, upon the motion of Samuel Adams, that the tea should be sent back, and that no duty should be paid on it. "The only way to get rid of it," said Young, "is to throw it overboard." At an adjourned meeting in the afternoon, Mr. Rotch entered his protest against the proceedings; but the meeting, without a dissenting voice, passed the significant vote that if Mr. Rotch entered the tea he would do so at his peril. Captain Hall was also cautioned not to allow any of the tea to be landed. To guard the ship during the night, a volunteer watch of twenty-five persons was appointed, under Captain Edward Proctor. "Out of great tenderness" to the consignees, the meeting adjourned to Tuesday morning, to allow further time for consultation. The answer, which was given jointly, then was that it was not in the power of the consignees to send the tea back; but they were ready to store it till they could hear from their constituents. Before action could be taken on this reply, Greenleaf, the Sheriff of Suffolk, entered with a proclamation from the Governor, charging the inhabitants with violating the good and wholesome laws of the province, and "warning, exhorting, and requiring them, and each of them there unlawfully assembled, forthwith to disperse."[2] This communication was received with hisses and a unanimous vote not to disperse. At this juncture, Copley the artist, son-in-law of Clarke, tendered his services as mediator between the people and the consignees, and was allowed two hours for the purpose; but after going to the Castle he returned with a report which was voted to be "not in the least degree satisfactory." In the afternoon, Rotch and Hall, yielding to the demands of the hour, agreed that the tea should return, without touching land or paying duty. A similar promise was obtained from the owners of two other tea-ships, which were daily expected; and resolutions were passed against such merchants as had even "inadvertently" imported tea while subject to duty. Armed patrols were appointed for the night; and six post-riders were selected to alarm the neighboring towns, if necessary. A report of the proceedings of the meeting was officially transmitted to every seaport in Massachusetts; also to New York and Philadelphia, and to England.[3]

In a short time the other tea-ships, the "Eleanor" and the "Beaver," arrived and, by order of the committee, were moored near the "Dartmouth" at Griffin's Wharf,[4] that one guard might answer for all. Under the revenue laws the ships could not be cleared in Boston with the tea on board, nor

---

the machinations of tyranny, stares you in the face. Every friend to his country, to himself and posterity, is now called upon to meet at Faneuil Hall at nine o'clock this day (at which time the bells will ring), to make a united and successful resistance to this last, worst, and most destructive measure of Administration."

*Boston Gazette,* Nov. 29, 1773; Wells's *Life of S. Adams,* ii. 110. [The original draft of the call to the committees of the neighboring towns, in Warren's hand, is owned by Mr. Bancroft. Frothingham's *Warren,* p. 255. — Ed.]

[1] Jonathan Williams was chosen moderator; and the business of the meeting was conducted by Adams, Hancock, Young, Molineux, and Warren.

[2] Hutchinson, *Massachusetts Bay,* iii. 432.

[3] For accounts of this meeting see *Boston Post-Boy, News-Letter,* and especially the *Gazette* for Dec. 6, 1773.

[4] Now Liverpool Wharf, near the foot of Pearl Street.

could they be entered in England; and, moreover, on the twentieth day from their arrival they would be liable to seizure. Whatever was done, therefore, must be done soon. The Patriot leaders were all sincerely anxious to have the tea returned to London peaceably, and they left nothing undone to accomplish this object. On the eleventh of December the owner of the "Dartmouth" was summoned before the committee, and asked why he had not kept his agreement to send his ship back with the tea. He replied that it was out of his power to do so. "The ship must go," was the answer. "The people of Boston and the neighboring towns absolutely require and expect it."[1] Hutchinson, in the meantime, had taken measures to prevent her sailing. No vessel was allowed to put to sea without his permit; the guns at the Castle were loaded, and Admiral Montagu had sent two war-ships to guard the passages out of the harbor.

The committees of the towns were in session on the thirteenth. On the fourteenth, two days before the time would expire, a meeting at the Old South again summoned Rotch and enjoined upon him, at his peril, to apply for a clearance. He did so, accompanied by several witnesses. The collector refused to give his answer until the next day, and the meeting adjourned to Thursday, the sixteenth, the last day of the twenty before confiscation would be legal. For two days the Boston committee of correspondence had been holding consultations of the greatest importance.

"That little body of stout-hearted men were making history that should endure for ages. Their secret deliberations, could they be exhumed from the dust of time, would present a curious page in the annals of Boston; but the seal of silence was upon the pen of the secretary, as well as upon the lips of the members."[2]

On Wednesday Rotch was again escorted to the Custom House, where both the collector and the comptroller "unequivocally and finally" refused to grant the "Dartmouth" a clearance unless her teas were discharged.

Thursday, December 16, came at last, — *dies irae, dies illa!* — and Boston calmly prepared to meet the issue. At ten o'clock the Old South was filled from an outside assemblage that included two thousand people from the surrounding country. Rotch appeared and reported that a clearance had been denied him. He was then directed as a last resort to protest at once against the decision of the Custom House, and apply to the Governor for a passport to go by the Castle. Hutchinson, evidently anticipating such an emergency, had found it convenient to be at his country-seat on Milton Hill,[3] where it would require considerable time to reach him. Rotch was instructed to make all haste, and report to the meeting in the afternoon. At three o'clock the number of people in and around the Old South was estimated at seven thousand, — by far the largest gathering ever seen in Boston. Addresses

[1] Bancroft, vi. 482.

[2] Wells's *Life of Samuel Adams*, ii. 119.

[3] [The mansion which is delineated in Bryant and Gay's *History of the United States*, iii. 372, as Hutchinson's country-seat, is not Hutchinson's house but another on Milton Hill. The true house was taken down not long since. — ED.]

were made by Samuel Adams, Young, Rowe, Quincy,[1] and others. "Who knows," said Rowe, "how tea will mingle with salt water?" a suggestion which was received with loud applause.[2] When the question was finally put to the vast assembly it was unanimously resolved that the tea should not be landed. It was now getting darker and darker, and the meeting-house could only be dimly lighted with a few candles; yet the people all remained, knowing that the great question must soon be decided. About six o'clock Rotch appeared and reported that he had waited on the Governor, but could not obtain a pass, as his vessel was not duly qualified. No sooner had he concluded than Samuel Adams arose and said: "This meeting can do nothing more to save the country."[3] Instantly a shout was heard at the porch; the war-whoop resounded, and a band of forty or fifty men, disguised as Indians, rushed by the door and hurried down toward the harbor,[4] followed by a throng of people; guards were carefully posted, according to previous arrangements, around Griffin's wharf to prevent the intrusion of spies. The "Mohawks," and some others accompanying them, sprang aboard the three tea-ships and emptied the contents of three hundred and forty-two chests of tea into the bay, "without the least injury to the vessels or any other property." No one interfered with them; no person was harmed; no tea was allowed to be carried away. There was no confusion, no noisy riot, no

---

[1] [The speech which Josiah Quincy, Jr. delivered at this meeting, Dec. 16, 1773, together with one of Otis in 1767, are the only reports at any length of all the speeches made in Boston public meetings from 1768 to 1775. Frothingham's *Warren*, p. 39. Quincy's *Life of Josiah Quincy, Jr.*, 2d ed. p. 124. Mr. Quincy's speech is preserved only in a letter which, after he had gone to England, he wrote to his wife from London, Dec. 14, 1774, and the words given by Gordon were copied from the manuscript still existing. It counselled moderation. *Mass. Hist. Soc. Proc.*, Dec. 16, 1873, Mr. Waterston's address. — ED.]

[2] Niles, *Principles and Acts of the Revolution*, pp. 485, 486.

[3] Francis Rotch's information before the privy council. [The moderator of this meeting was William Phillips Savage. His portrait is owned by Mr. G. H. Emery. The original minutes, in the hand of William Cooper, of the meetings from Nov. 29, 1773, are preserved among the papers in the Charity Building. They show the names of the watch of twenty-five men, under Captain Proctor, who were to guard the ships that night; and later each successive watch was empowered to appoint its successors for the following night. The final report of Mr. Rotch is entered in the minutes for December 16, as follows: —

"Mr. Rotch attended and informed that he had demanded a pass for his vessel of the Governor, who answered that he was willing to grant anything consistent with the laws and his duty to

the King, but that he could not give a pass unless the vessel was properly qualified from the Custom House; that he should make no distinction between this and any other vessel, provided she was properly cleared.

"Mr. Rotch was then asked whether he would send his vessel back with the tea under her present circumstances; he answered that he could not possibly comply, as he apprehended it would be to his risk. He was further asked whether he would land the tea; he answered he had no business with it unless he was properly called upon to do it, when he should attempt a compliance for his own security.

"*Voted*, that this meeting be dissolved; and it was accordingly dissolved."

Here the minutes end, the remaining leaves of the book being blank. — ED.]

[4] [The conclave which had decided upon this movement had been held in the back office of Edes & Gill's printing house, on the site of the present *Daily Advertiser* building. A room over the office was often the meeting place of the Patriots, and the frequenters got to be known as the Long-Room Club. Drake, *Landmarks*, p. 81. There is some reason to believe that this was the office of Josiah Quincy, Jr. A letter about the punch-bowl used by the Patriots before going to the wharf is given in *Mass. Hist. Soc. Proc.*, December, 1871. Lossing, *Field-Book of the Revolution*, i. 499, gives the portrait of David Kinnison, the last survivor of the "Mohawks." — ED.]

infuriated mob.  The multitude stood by and looked on in solemn silence while the weird-looking figures,[1] made distinctly visible in the moonlight, removed the hatches, tore open the chests, and threw the entire cargo overboard.  This strange spectacle lasted about three hours, and then the people all went home and the town was as quiet as if nothing had happened.  The next day fragments of the tea were seen strewn along the Dorchester shore, carried thither by the wind and tide.[2]  A formal declaration of the transaction was drawn up by the Boston committee; and Paul Revere was sent with despatches to New York and Philadelphia, where the news was received with the greatest demonstrations of joy.[3]  In Boston the feeling was that of intense satisfaction proceeding from the consciousness of having exhausted every possible measure of legal redress before undertaking this bold and novel mode of asserting the rights of the people.[4]  "We do console ourselves," said John Scollay, one of the selectmen, and an actor in the scene, "that we have acted constitutionally."[5]  "This is the most magnificent movement of all," said John Adams.[6]  "There

[1] The names of the actors in this scene, as well as of those who planned it, were not divulged till after the Revolutionary War.  It is supposed that about one hundred and forty persons were engaged in it.  [The "Dartmouth's" journal says one thousand people came on the wharf.  The party actually boarding the ships has been estimated from seventeen to thirty, the former number being all that have been identified.  See Frothingham in *Mass. Hist. Soc. Proc.*, Dec. 16, 1873, who thinks that the list given in Hewes's book is not accurate as respects those who boarded the ships.  "Several of the party have been identified, but the claims presented for others are doubtful."  John Adams refused to have the names given him.  (*Works*, ii. 334.)  Captain Henry Purkitt, who is called the last survivor of the party, died March 3, 1846, aged ninety-one.  As to Hewes, see also Loring's *Hundred Boston Orators*, p. 554 — Ed.]

[2] Barry, ii. 473.  [A small quantity of it is preserved in a phial in the Mass. Hist. Society's cabinet.  Thomas Newell records in his diary, Jan. 1, 1774: "Last evening a number of persons went over to Dorchester and brought from thence part of a chest of tea, and burnt it in our Common the same evening."  A fourth vessel of the tea-fleet was wrecked on the back side of Cape Cod.  The Boston committee immediately sent a message in that direction.  "The people of the Cape will we hope behave with propriety, and as becomes men resolved to serve their country."  We next hear of this tea in a letter from Samuel Adams to James Warren, Jan. 10, 1774: "The tea which was cast on shore at the

Cape has been brought up, and after much consultation landed at Castle William, the safe asylum for our inveterate enemies. . . . It is said that the Indians this way, if they had suspected the Marshpee tribe would have been so sick at the knee, would have marched on snow-shoes to have done the business for them."  It seems that Clarke, one of the consignees, had despatched a lighter and brought the chests off.  *Mass. Hist. Soc. Proc.*, Dec. 16, 1873.  Vessels subsequently arriving were examined; and in March, 1774, twenty-eight and a half chests were similarly disposed of by similar "Indians." — Ed.]

[3] [Revere returned from this mission December 27; and bringing word that Governor Tryon had engaged to send the New York tea-ships back, all the Boston bells were rung the next morning.  *Thomas Newell's Diary.* — Ed.]

[4] "Fast spread the tempest's darkening pall;
    The mighty realms were troubled;
The storm broke loose, but first of all
    The Boston teapot bubbled.

"The lurid morning shall reveal
    A fire no king can smother,
When British flint and Boston steel,
    Have clashed against each other!"
                                    O. W. HOLMES.

[5] Letter to Arthur Lee, Dec. 23, 1773.

[6] Diary, Dec. 17, 1773.  [Two pages of this diary, of which the accompanying *fac-simile* is a

1773 Dec 17th Last Night 3 Cargoes of Bohea Tea were emptied into the Sea: This Morning a Man of War Sails. —

This is the most magnificent Movement of all. —

is a dignity, a majesty, a sublimity, in this last effort of the Patriots that I greatly admire." [1]

The blow was now struck; the deed was done; and there was no retreat. The enemies of liberty talked of treason, arrests, and executions; but the Patriots almost everywhere rejoiced, and pledged themselves to support the common cause. Independence was now openly advocated; a congress was called for; and "Union" was the cry from New England to Carolina.[2]

When the news of the destruction of the tea reached England it produced a profound sensation, both in Government circles and among the people. Coercion was at once resolved upon as the only means of check-

fragment, are given in the *Mass. Hist. Soc. Proc.*, Dec. 16, 1873. — ED.]

[1] Charles Waterton, the enterprising traveller and naturalist, of Walton Hall, Wakefield, Yorkshire, makes a humorous reference to the Tea-Party, in his autobiography, written between 1812 and 1824: "It is but some forty years ago our western brother had a dispute with his nurse about a cup of tea. She wanted to force the boy to drink it according to her own receipt. He said he did not like it, and that it absolutely made him ill. After a good deal of sparring, she took up the birch rod and began to whip him with uncommon severity. He turned upon her in self-defence, showed her to the outside of the nursery door, and never more allowed her to meddle with his affairs."

[2] [Among the contemporary sources for the understanding of these transactions may be named the following: G. R. T. Hewes, who was one of the participants, with the aid of B. B. Thacher, prepared *Traits of the Tea-Party*, N. Y. 1835 (see also *Retrospect of the Boston Tea-Party with a Memoir of Hewes*, by a citizen of New York, N. Y. 1834. *Brinley Catalogue*, Nos. 1681 and 1682); and in this book the names of fifty-eight actors in the scene are given. The names inscribed on the monument of Captain Peter Slater (who was one of the party) in Hope Cemetery, New Worcester, are sixty-three in number. Both lists include Moses Grant, William Molineaux, Paul Revere, G. T. R. Hewes, Thomas Melville, Samuel Sprague, Jonathan Hunnewell, John Prince, John Russell. (*Massachusetts Spy*, Dec. 16, 1873.) Sprague was the father of Charles Sprague; Russell was the father of Benjamin Russell. Hewes lived at the Bull's Head, an old house on the northeast corner of Water and Congress streets. He died Nov. 5, 1840, at ninety-eight. There are letters from Boston in 4 *Mass. Hist. Coll.* iv. 373; as also the examination of Dr. Williamson before the King's council, Feb. 19, 1774. A paper, "Information of Hugh Williamson" is in the Sparks MSS. Admiral Montagu, writing Dec. 17, 1773, to the Lords of the Admiralty, says he

was never called upon for assistance, and he could easily have prevented the execution of the plan; and the *Evening Post*, May 16, 1774, ventured from the admiral's admission to draw the conclusion that Hutchinson and his party connived at the business. The first accounts received in England are given in the *Gentleman's Magazine*, 1774, p. 26. An account is in the *Boston Gazette*, Dec. 20, 1773, or Buckingham's *Reminiscences*, i. 169; a contemporary record in Andrews's letters in *Mass. Hist. Soc. Proc.*, 1865, p. 325; Thomas Newell's Diary in *Mass. Hist. Soc. Proc.*, October, 1877; contemporary verses in *Mag. of Amer. History*, March, 1880; Hutchinson's narrative is in his *Massachusetts Bay*, iii. 430. Hutchinson's papers in the State House throw much light on these disturbed times, and some of his letters are copied by Frothingham in his paper in the *Mass. Hist. Soc. Proc.*, December, 1873. His interview with the king, July 1, 1774, after his return to England, as reported in his journal, and covering these transactions, has only of late years been made public. *Mass. Hist. Soc. Proc.*, October, 1877, p. 326. Other contemporary documents will be found in Force's *American Archives*, i.; Niles's *Principles and Acts of the Revolution;* Franklin's *Works*, viii.; John Adams's *Works*, ii. 323, 334, and ix. 333. An appeal of "Scævola" to the commissioners appointed for the sale of tea in America was printed as a broadside, and a copy is in the Sparks MSS. xlix. vol. ii. p. 115. Of the eclectic later accounts the fullest is in Frothingham's *Life of Warren*, ch. ix.; and in his paper in *Mass. Hist. Soc. Proc.*, Dec. 16, 1873, where will be found the contributions of others to that commemorative occasion. See also Bancroft, vi. ch. 1.; Barry, *Massachusetts*, ii. ch. xiv. and xv.; Wells's *Sam. Adams*, ii.; Tudor's *Otis*, ch. xxi.; Snow's *Boston;* Niles's *Register*, 1827, p. 75; Lossing's *Field-Book;* and *Harper's Monthly*, iv. Also James Kimball in *Essex Institute Proceedings*. The English writers are May's *Constitutional History of England*, ii. 521; Massey's *England*, ii. ch. xviii.; Fitzmaurice's *Shelburne*, ii.; Macknight's *Burke*, ii. ch. xx.; and the usual general historians. — ED.]

ing the unruly and defiant spirit which had become dominant in Boston.
On March 7 the King, in addressing Parliament, accused the Americans of
attempting to injure British commerce and to subvert its constitution.
The message was accompanied with a mass of papers and letters.[1] Lord
North demanded additional powers in order to re-establish peace.    The
question at issue, it was said, was whether the colonies were or were not
the colonies of Great Britain.   If they were, they should be held firmly;
if they were not, they should be released.   Upon this question there was,
just at this time, great unanimity in England.   The authority of the Crown,
it was urged, must be maintained at all hazards.   Any act in violation of
that must be punished.   Even the party in opposition yielded much upon
this point.   Thus the ministry were fully prepared to introduce the most
pronounced penal measures; and on the eighteenth, Lord North, disre-
garding constitutional forms, which forbid that any should be condemned
unheard, brought in the famous Boston Port Bill, — a measure for suspend-
ing the trade and closing the harbor of Boston during the king's pleasure,
and enforcing the act by the joint operations of an army and a fleet.[2]   The
bill was stoutly opposed by Burke, Barré, Dowdeswell, Pownall, and others;
but in two weeks it passed through the various stages and was carried
without a division in the Commons, and unanimously in the Lords, and
became a law March 31 by the royal assent.   This act was to go into effect
on the first day of June.   It took away from Boston the privilege of landing and discharging, as well as of loading and shipping, all goods, wares,
and merchandise.[3]   It constituted Marblehead a port of entry, and Salem
the seat of government.   As if this were not enough, Lord North now
brought in within a month a series of measures, compared with which all
that had gone before was mild and legitimate.   The ministry seemed determined to wreak their vengeance upon the devoted head of Massachusetts; and nothing was too arbitrary, radical, or revolutionary for them to
recommend.   Up to this point there might have been a way of reconcili-
ation.   The cruel and exasperating Port Bill would probably have been
withdrawn upon certain easy and perhaps reasonable conditions.   The tea-
tax and its preamble, which gave such offence to the colonists, might have
been repealed; indeed an attempt to do so was made on April 19, when
Edmund Burke made his ever memorable speech.[4]   But when the penal

---

[1] These letters were from Hutchinson and
other royal governors, and from Admiral Montagu and the consignees of the tea, accompanied by a large number of pamphlets, mani-
festoes, handbills, etc., issued in the colonies.
[The king and council had already, Feb. 7,
1774, considered the petition of the House of
Representatives for the removal of Hutchinson
and Oliver, and had dismissed the charges " as
groundless, vexatious, and scandalous, and calculated only for the seditious purpose of keeping up a spirit of clamour and discontent."   The
official copy sent to Arthur Lee, No. 3 Garden

Court, Temple, is in the Lee Papers, University
of Virginia. — ED.]

[2] "The offence of the Americans," it was
said in the course of the debate, "is flagitious.
The town of Boston ought to be knocked about
their ears and destroyed.   *Delenda est Carthago.*
You will never meet with proper obedience to
the laws of this country until you have destroyed that nest of locusts." — *Mass. Gazette,*
May 19, 1774.

[3] [See Sargent's *Dealings with the Dead,* i.
153. — ED.]

[4] *Works,* Boston, 1865, vol. ii. p. 1.

measures, commonly known as the Regulation or Reconstructive Acts, were passed, a fatal blow was struck at the American system of local self-government, and the conflict was beyond recall.

These acts, which passed in rapid succession during the month of April, were for the purpose of "regulating the government of the Province of Massachusetts Bay."[1] The speech of Lord George Germain, on the introduction of the bill, shows how sadly ignorance concerning America, and contempt for her institutions, had pervaded England at this time. Speaking of North's plan to punish the people of Massachusetts, he said: —

"Nor can I think he will do a better thing than to put an end to their town-meetings. I would not have men of a mercantile cast every day collecting themselves together and debating about political matters. I would have them follow their occupations as merchants, and not consider themselves as ministers of that country. . . . I would wish to see the Council in that country similar to the House of Lords in this. . . . The whole are the proceedings of a tumultuous and riotous rabble, who ought, if they had the least prudence, to follow their mercantile employments, and not trouble themselves with politics and government which they do not understand."

When he had finished this remarkable speech, Lord North arose and said: "I thank the noble lord for every proposition he has held out. They are worthy of a great mind, and such as ought to be adopted."[2]

For the purpose of strengthening the executive authority, these Regulation Acts, without giving any hearing to the Province, provided, —

1. In total violation of the charter, that the councillors who had been chosen hitherto by the Legislature should be appointed by the king, and hold at his pleasure. The superior judges were to hold at the will of the king, and be dependent upon him for their salaries; and the inferior judges were to be removable at the discretion of the royal governor. The sheriffs were to be appointed and removed by the executive; and the juries were to be selected by the dependent sheriffs. Town-meetings were to be abolished, except for the election of officers, or by the special permission of the Governor. This bill passed by a vote of more than three to one.

2. Magistrates, revenue officers, and soldiers, charged with capital offences, could be tried in England or Nova Scotia. This bill passed by a vote of more than four to one.

3. A military act provided for the quartering of troops upon the towns.[3]

These oppressive edicts, said the Massachusetts committee in their circular, were only what might have been expected from a Parliament claiming[4] the right to make laws binding the colonies "in all cases whatsoever."

[1] [The debates are given in 4 Force's American Archives, i. — Ed.]

[2] Parliamentary History, xvii. pp. 1192–1195. Also Boston newspapers of May 19 and 23, 1774.

[3] Boston Post-Boy, June 6 and 13, 1774. Gordon, American Revolution, i. 232–235. Mahon, History of England, vi. 5, 6. Bancroft, vi. 525, 526. Frothingham, Rise of the Republic, pp. 345–347. Dana, Oration at Lexington, April 19, 1875.

[4] In the declaratory act. See earlier in this chapter.

The news of the Port Act created, as may well be supposed, the greatest indignation in the colonies; but Boston stood firm, and the other seaports refused to profit by her patriotic sufferings.

In May Hutchinson was recalled, to the great relief of the people of the province; and Thomas Gage, Commander-in-chief of the continent, was appointed also Governor of Massachusetts. In all the political agitations in the colonies thus far, Gage had behaved so discreetly as an officer that he enjoyed a considerable share of public confidence. After a lengthy interview with his predecessor at Castle William, he landed at Long Wharf, on May 17, saluted by the ships and batteries, and received by the civil officers of the province. The cadets, under Colonel Hancock, performed escort duty, and the council presented a loyal address at the State House.[1] A public dinner followed at Faneuil Hall.[2] Undoubtedly this welcome given to Gage was owing, in part, to the delight of the people at the retirement of Hutchinson.[3] But it soon appeared that the new Governor, with many excellent traits, was not the man to reconcile or to subdue, if indeed any such man could have been found in the whole British service at this critical moment. It devolved upon Gage to close the port of Boston and to enforce the measures of the odious Regulation Acts. The blockade of the harbor began on the first day of June, after which all intercourse by water, even among the nearest islands or from pier to pier, was rigidly forbidden. Not a ferry could ply to Charlestown, nor a scow to Dorchester. Warehouses were at once useless, wharves deserted, and ordinary business prostrated. All classes felt the scourge of the oppressor; yet there was no regret at the position which the town had deliberately taken in defence of its constitutional rights. These were dearer to the inhabitants than property or peace or even life itself, as was shortly to be proved. Expressions of sympathy poured in from all quarters. Supplies of food and money were generously sent from the other colonies as well as from the neighboring towns.[4] Salem and Marblehead scorned to profit

---

[1] ["The Town House is fitted up in the most elegant manner, with the whole of the outside painted of a stone color, which gives it a fine appearance."—June, 1773, in *Mass. Hist. Soc. Proc.*, July, 1865, p. 321. Hancock had the previous March, 1774, delivered the usual Massacre oration, which in the opinion of some was written by Samuel Adams. *John Adams's Works*, ii. 332; Wells's *S. Adams*.—ED.]

[2] [Gage at this "elegant entertainment gave 'Governor Hutchinson' as a toast, which was received by a general hiss."—*Mass. Hist. Soc. Proc.*, 1865, p. 328.—ED.]

[3] [The friends of Hutchinson and the prerogative made themselves conspicuous by an address on his leaving the province, and a list of the "addressers" is given in *Mass. Hist. Soc. Proc.*, October, 1870.—ED.]

[4] [There are at the City Hall various lists of donations received at this time, with the records of the donation committee. See Vol. I. p. xx. The correspondence of this committee is in 4 *Mass. Hist. Coll.*, iv. Colonel A. H. Hoyt has given an account of these gifts in the *N. E. Hist. and Geneal. Reg.*, July, 1876. A subscription-list of contributions raised in Virginia in 1774, for the "distressed inhabitants of Boston," is printed in the *Mass. Hist. Soc. Proc.*, December, 1857. When the Marbleheaders sent in provisions for the Boston poor, they were refused passage for them by water, and an expensive land-carriage of twenty-eight miles was rendered necessary, as even a ferry passage was refused. *Mass. Hist. Soc. Proc.*, 1865, p. 336. Benefactors in South Carolina and Connecticut were equally compelled to pay for a land passage.—ED.]

by the sufferings of Boston, and offered the free use of their wharves and stores.[1]

The committee of correspondence assumed with much ability the arduous and responsible task of guiding public affairs at this crisis. "A solemn league and covenant" to suspend all commercial intercourse with England, and forego the use of all British merchandise, was forwarded to every town in the province; and the names of those who refused to sign it were to be published. The first act of the Legislature at Salem was to protest against the illegal order for its removal. The House of Representatives was the fullest ever known in the country, one hundred and twenty-nine being present. It was for them to fix the time and place for the proposed meeting of the Continental Congress, for which Samuel Adams and his coadjutors were diligently laboring.[2] While they were sitting with closed doors a message came from the Governor dissolving the Assembly, but not until its important work had been done.[3] Baffled in his purposes and chagrined at the success of the Patriots, Gage, without consulting the council, issued his foolish and malignant proclamation against the combination not to purchase British goods. He denounced it as "unwarrantable, hostile, and traitorous;" its subscribers as "open and declared enemies of the King and Parliament;" and he "enjoined and commanded all magistrates and other officers . . . to apprehend and secure for trial all persons who might publish or sign, or invite others to sign, the covenant." It was known that the Governor was endeavoring to fasten charges of rebellion upon several of the popular leaders, in order to secure their arrest; but his plans did not succeed.

In August the Regulation Acts were officially received by Gage and immediately put into effect, sweeping away the long cherished Charter of Massachusetts, and precipitating the irreversible choice between submission and resistance. Samuel Adams wrote:[4] —

"Boston suffers with dignity. If Britain by her multiplied oppressions accelerates the independency of her colonies, whom will she have to blame but herself? It is

[1] [In 1774 John Kneeland printed at Boston a part of Thomas Prince's sermon on the destruction of D'Anville's fleet in 1746, "with a view to encourage and animate the people of God to put their trust in him, under the severe and keen distresses now taking place, by the rigorous execution of the Port Bill." Ellis Gray, writing from Boston at this time to a friend in Jamaica, somewhat drolly apologizes for his slack correspondence on the ground that he lived "seventeen miles from a sea-port," — referring to Salem and Marblehead. See *Mass. Hist. Soc. Proc.*, March, 1876, p. 315. The *Royal Amer. Mag.*, June, 1774, has one of Revere's satires on the Port Bill, in "The Able Doctor, or America swallowing the bitter Draught." The same magazine for May contains the act for blockading the port of Boston. An expression of the prevailing feeling is found in Andrews's letters. *Mass. Hist. Soc. Proc.*, 1865, p. 327. — Ed.]

[2] [C. M. Endicott's *Leslie's Retreat*, p. 9. — Ed.]

[3] The Congress was appointed to meet in September, at Philadelphia, and the Massachusetts delegates were Bowdoin (who, however, could not attend), Samuel Adams, John Adams, Cushing, and Robert Treat Paine. [This Congress sat in Philadelphia from September 5 to October 26. The idea of it is said to have originated with Franklin. Its proceedings, issued in Philadelphia, were at once reprinted in Boston. Numerous references are given in Winsor's *Handbook*, pp. 16–19. — Ed.]

[4] Letters to William Checkley and Charles Thomson, June 1 and 2, 1774.

a consolatory thought that an empire is rising in America. . . . Our people think
they should pursue the line of the Constitution as far as they can; and if they are
driven from it they can with propriety and justice appeal to God and to the world.
. . . Nothing is more foreign to our hearts than a spirit of rebellion. Would to God
they all, even our enemies, knew the warm attachment we have for Great Britain,
notwithstanding we have been contending these ten years with them for our rights!"

That attachment was ruthlessly severed by the operation of the new acts.
"We were not the revolutionists," says Mr. Dana.[1] "The King and Parliament were the revolutionists. They were the radical innovators. We were
the conservators of existing institutions. They were seeking to overthrow
and reconstruct on a theory of parliamentary omnipotence. . . . We broke
no chain."

Boston was now occupied by a large military force. The Fourth, Fifth,
Thirty-eighth, and Forty-third regiments, together with twenty-two pieces
of cannon and three companies of artillery, were encamped on the Common.[2]
The Welsh Fusileers were encamped on Fort Hill, and several companies
of the Sixty-fourth were at Castle William, where most of the powder and
other stores had been removed from New York. The Fifty-ninth was encamped at Salem, to protect the meetings of the new mandamus council;
and two companies of the Sixty-fourth were at Danvers, to cover the Govern-
or's residence.[3] The camp at Boston was, in the absence of Gage, under
command of Earl Percy, who had recently arrived with Colonels Pigott and
Jones. Lord Percy describes the situation with some minuteness in his
letters written to friends in England at this time:[4] —

"The people, by all accounts, are extremely violent and wrong-headed; so much
so that I fear we shall be obliged to come to extremities." "One thing I will be bold

[1] Oration at Lexington. April 19, 1875.

[2] [We get a glimpse of the British camp at
this time in the privately printed Memoir and
Letters of Captain W. Glanville Evelyn of the
Fourth Regiment ("King's Own"), which was
printed in 1879 at Oxford, edited by G. D. Scull.
This officer joined his regiment in June, 1774, and
wrote home sundry letters here preserved, in
which the provincials appear as "rascals and
poltroons." In December he was quartered in a
house, and, having "laid in a good stock of Port
and Madeira, hoped to spend the winter as well
as our neighbors." He speaks of Sam Adams
"as moving and directing this immense continent, — a man of ordinary birth and desperate
fortune, who, by his abilities and talent for factious intrigue, has made himself of some consequence; whose political existence depends upon
the continuance of the present dispute, and who
must sink into insignificancy and beggary the
moment it ceases" (p. 46). "Hancock is a poor
contemptible fool, led about by Adams." Dr.
Holmes draws the picture of the Common at
this time: —

"And over all the open green
Where grazed of late the harmless kine,
The cannon's deepening ruts are seen,
The war horse stamps, the bayonets shine."

John Andrews, writing of the delegation to
the Congress of September, 1774, says: "Robert
Treat Paine set out with the committee this
morning [Aug. 10]. They made a very respectable parade in sight of five of the regiments
encamped on the Common; being in a coach
and four, preceded by two white servants well
mounted and armed, with four blacks behind in
livery, two on horseback and two footmen." —
Mass. Hist. Soc. Proc., July, 1805, p 339. — ED.]

[3] [Here, at the country residence of Robert
Hooper, "King Hooper" of Marblehead, Gage
had his headquarters for a while, Salem being
then, under the Port Bill, the capital. On Aug.
27, 1774, Gage left Danvers and moved his
headquarters to Boston, and the Fifty-ninth
and Sixty-fourth regiments soon followed him,
the former taking post on Boston Neck to
throw up entrenchments there. — ED.]

[4] Private letters in possession of his Grace
the Duke of Northumberland, and copied, by

to say, which is, that till you make their committees of correspondence and congresses with the other colonies high treason, and try them for it in England, you never must expect perfect obedience from this to the mother country." "This is the most beautiful country I ever saw in my life, and if the people were only like it we should do very well. Everything, however, is as yet quiet, but they threaten much. Not that I believe they dare act." " We have at last got the new acts, and twenty-six of the new council have accepted and are sworn in ; but for my own part, I doubt whether they will be more active than the old ones. Such a set of timid creatures I never did see. Those of the new council that live at any distance from town have remained here ever since they took the oaths, and are, I am told, afraid to go home again. As for the opposite party, they are arming and exercising all over the country. . . . Their method of eluding that part of the act which relates to the town-meetings is strongly characteristic of the people. They say that since the town-meetings are forbid by the act, they shall not hold them ; but as they do not see any mention made of county meetings, they shall hold them for the future. They therefore go a mile out of town, do just the same business there they formerly did in Boston, call it a county meeting, and so elude the act.[1] In short, I am certain that it will require a great length of time, much steadiness, and many troops, to re-establish good order and government. I plainly foresee that there is not a new councillor or magistrate who will dare to act without at least a regiment at his heels ; and it is not quite clear to me that he will even act then as he ought to do." "The delegates from this province are set out (August 21) to meet the General Congress at Philadelphia. They talk much of non-importation, and an agreement between the colonies. . . . I flatter myself, however, that instead of agreeing to anything, they will all go by the ears together at this Congress. If they don't, there will be more work cut out for administration in America than perhaps they are aware of."

It soon appeared that the new acts were powerless to accomplish the end contemplated by the Government. With all the support furnished by a royal governor, royal judges, and a royal army, the courts could not sit, jurors would not serve, and the people would not obey. Sheriffs were timid, councillors resigned their places and soldiers deserted. Meanwhile the colonists were busy, maturing their plans in clubs, caucuses, and conventions. Whether these were legal or illegal under the new act, they did not stop to inquire.

permission, by the present writer. Hugh Earl Percy was born August 25, 1742. In early life he adopted the military profession, and served under Prince Ferdinand of Brunswick in the Seven Years' War. He arrived in Boston July 5, 1774, with the Fifth Regiment of foot, and remained in the service in this country until May 3, 1777, when he returned to England with the rank of lieut.-general in North America. He was especially prominent at Lexington, and in the attack on Fort Washington, at King's Bridge. Soon after his return to England, he was selected to head a commission to offer terms of conciliation to Congress ; but, owing to a division in the British Cabinet, Lord Percy declined the offer, and the project was abandoned. After this, he represented the city of Westminster in Parliament until the year 1786, when he succeeded his father as Duke of Northumberland. For many years his time was chiefly employed in improving his princely estates. During the war with France, he raised from among his tenantry a corps of fifteen hundred men, called the "Percy Yeomanry," the whole corps being paid, clothed, and maintained by himself. He was a Knight of the Garter, a member of several learned societies, and the recipient of many of the highest honors of the realm. He died at Northumberland House, London, July 10, 1817, in the seventy-fifth year of his age, and was buried in St. Nicholas Chapel, Westminster Abbey.

[1] [This explains the somewhat strange appellation of the "Suffolk Resolves," mentioned later in the text. ED.]

VOL. III. — 8.

No act of Parliament, they maintained, could impose restrictions upon those ancient and chartered rights which they had always enjoyed. With this

¹ This cut follows an engraving by V. Green, executed in London, in 1777, and measuring 18 × 12½ inches. The plate was engraved from a portrait presented by the Duke of Northumberland, July 30, 1776, to the magistrates of Westminster, and placed in the council chamber of

conviction they had resisted the injustice of the Stamp Act and the Tea Act, and they were not the men to yield now to a tyranny far greater than either.

THE WARREN HOUSE IN ROXBURY.[1]

The Regulating Act had not been long in operation before the popular resistance which it encountered found appropriate expression in the famous Suffolk Resolves drawn up by Warren, who acted as a kind of director-general during the absence of Samuel Adams at Philadelphia. These resolves,

their Guild Hall in commemoration of Lord Percy's public services. The portrait was evidently a duplicate of the one by Pompeio Battoni, now at Alnwick Castle, a copy of which was made in 1879 by order of the present Duke and presented, through the writer of this chapter, to the Town of Lexington. Another likeness of Earl Percy, taken later in life, may be seen with a brief account in Captain Evelyn's *Memoir and Letters*, p. 127

[1] [This cut follows a painting now owned by the wife of Dr Buckminster Brown, of Boston, a descendant of General Warren. The house was built in 1720 by Joseph Warren, the General's grandfather. It was used as quarters for Colonel David Brewer's regiment during the summer of 1775. The late Dr. John C. Warren acquired the estate in 1805; and selling off all but the house in 1833, he built, in 1846, the present stone cottage on the site. (*Life of Dr. John Warren*, ch. i.) In the old house (of which another view, as well as one of the present cottage, is given in Drake's *Town of Roxbury*, p. 213) Joseph Warren was born, in 1741; but at this time he lived on Hanover Street, where the American House now stands, hiring the mansion house of Joseph Green, which stood there. *Mass. Hist. Soc. Proc.*, 1875, p. 101. Ellis Ames, Esq., has parts of Warren's day-book between January, 1774, and January, 1775, showing the extent of his medical practice. Frothingham, *Life of Warren*, p. 167. — ED.]

nineteen in number,[1] were adopted in September by the Suffolk convention, which met first at Dedham,[2] and then, by adjournment, at Milton.[3]   They

*In Committee of Safety Cambridge May 14. 1775*

*Jos Warren Ch*

declared that the sovereign who breaks his compact with his subjects forfeits their allegiance.   They arraigned the unconstitutional acts of Parliament,

[1] Given in Frothingham's *Warren*, pp. 365–367, and Appendix i.
[2] At the house of Richard Woodward.
[3] At the house of Daniel Vose.
[4] [This cut follows a painting by Copley, now

in the possession of Dr. Buckminster Brown, of Boston, who kindly allowed it to be photographed for the engraver's use.  Perkins, in his *Copley's Life and Paintings*, p. 113, says: "The canvas is about five feet long by four wide, and the color-

and rejected all officers appointed under their authority. They directed collectors of taxes to pay over no money to the royal treasurer. They advised the towns to choose their officers of militia from the friends of the people. They favored a Provincial Congress, and promised respect and submission to the Continental Congress. They determined to act upon the defensive as long as reason and self-preservation would permit, "but no longer." They threatened to seize every Crown officer in the province as hostages if the Governor should arrest any one for political reasons. They

ing is very beautiful. It was one of Copley's last portraits before he left Boston for Europe in 1774, and as a piece of artistic skill, as well as for its historic interest, has been pronounced by good judges to be one of the most valuable of Copley's portraits in this country. It was painted while General Warren was the presiding officer of the Massachusetts Congress." The sitter and the artist were intimate friends, and the portrait was painted for General Warren's children, and has always been in the possession of some branch of the family. This portrait, with that of Mrs. Warren, by the same artist, was loaned to Mr. W. W. Corcoran for exhibition in his gallery at Washington, D. C. There is extant a letter from Lord Lyndhurst in which he makes inquiries respecting it, in reference, it is supposed, to the possibility of securing it for an English collection. These paintings have been in Boston since the spring of 1876, and have never before been reproduced. That of Mrs. Warren, of the same size, was probably painted three or four years previously. She died in 1773, at the age of twenty-six.

The familiar engraved likeness of General Warren, following another Copley, 29 x 24 inches, in citizen's dress, showing one hand, was originally owned by General Arnold Welles who married Warren's daughter, from whom it passed to the late Dr. John C. Warren, and is now owned by his grandson of the same name. Another half-length by Copley, belonging to the city, is now in the Art Museum. Early engravings of Warren are to be found in the *Impartial History of the War*, Boston edition (engraved by J. Norman, full-length, and showing the battle of Bunker Hill in the background), and in the *Boston Magazine*, May, 1784, following Copley's picture and engraved by J. Norman. A colored engraving resembling Copley's likeness was also frequently seen, and a copy is now preserved in the pavilion on Bunker Hill. A portrait statue, based on Copley's likeness, and executed by Henry Dexter, was erected in this pavilion in 1857, when dedicatory services took place on the anniversary of the battle, with an address by Edward Everett. An engraving of the statue is given in the commemorative volume which was issued at the time by the Bunker Hill Monument Association. See

also George Washington Warren's *History of the Bunker Hill Monument Association.*

General Warren left four children, two sons and two daughters. The sons died in early manhood. One daughter married General Arnold Welles, of Boston, and died without children. The second daughter was twice married: first to Mr. Lyman, of Northampton, and second to Judge Newcomb, of Greenfield, Mass. This daughter died in 1820, leaving one son, Joseph Warren Newcomb, who had two children, a son and daughter. The descendants of General Warren now living are a great-grand-daughter, who is married and lives in Boston, and a great-great-grandson, who is a cadet at West Point.

A sumptuous volume, *Genealogy of Warren*, by Dr. John C. Warren, was printed in Boston, in 1854, to show the connections of the Patriot both in this country and presumably and possibly in England. For an account of the papers of General Warren, see *Life of John C. Warren*, i. 217. One of Pendleton's earliest lithographs was of Warren's portrait, which appeared with a memoir in the *Boston Monthly Magazine*, June, 1826.

Abigail Adams repeats a story of an intended indignity to the body of Warren after his fall at Bunker Hill, from which he was saved by his Freemasonry affiliations. (*Familiar Letters*, p. 91.) On the repossession of Boston after the siege, the body was exhumed from the spot where he fell; and after an oration pronounced over it by Perez Morton (which was printed and is quoted in Loring's *Hundred Boston Orators*, p. 127*), it was deposited in the Minot tomb in the Granary Burying-ground; and in 1825 was removed to a tomb beneath St. Paul's, whence, at a later day, the remains were again removed to Forest Hills cemetery. Shurtleff's *Description of Boston*, p. 251. See an account of some relics of Warren by J. S. Loring in the *Hist. Mag.*, December, 1857. His sword is in the possession of Dr. John Collins Warren. *Mass. Hist. Soc. Proc.*, September, 1866, p. 348. — ED.]

* Also reprinted in a *Biographical Sketch of General Joseph Warren, embracing his Boston Orations of 1772 and 1775: together with the Eulogy pronounced by Perez Morton, in 1776*. By a Bostonian. Boston: 1857.

also arranged a system of couriers to carry messages to town officers and corresponding committees. They earnestly advocated the well known American principles of social order as the basis of all political action; exhorted all persons to abstain from riots and all attacks upon the property of any person whatsoever; and urged their countrymen to convince their "enemies that in a contest so important, in a cause so solemn, their conduct should be such as to merit the approbation of the wise, and the admiration of the brave and free of every age and of every country." For boldness and practical utility these resolves surpassed anything that had been promulgated in America. They were sent by Paul Revere as a memorial to the Congress at Philadelphia, where they were received with great applause, and recommended to the whole country.

Gage, perceiving that the time for reasoning had passed, applied[1] for more troops, seized the powder belonging to the Province,[2] and began the construction of fortifications on the Neck, near the Roxbury line, commanding the only land entrance which Boston had.[3] Beyond the limits of Boston

---

[1] [Correspondence of Gage at this time with Lord Dartmouth is in the *Mass. Hist. Soc. Proc.*, 1876, p. 347. See also *Life of Lord Barrington*. — ED.]

[2] [On September 1, 1774, Gage sent 260 soldiers, who embarked in boats at Long Wharf, to seize the Province's store of powder, which was kept in the old mill on the road from Winter Hill to Arlington. William Brattle, at that time commanding the Province militia, had instigated the movement. It was successful, and the troops returned bringing not only the powder, but two field-pieces which they had seized in Cambridge. This theft was soon avenged. An artillery company had been organized by Capt. David Mason in 1763, and was known commonly as "the train," and attached to the Boston regiment. Its command had passed in 1768 to Lieutenant Adino Paddock, who was a good drill master, and who

*Adino Paddock*

1772

derived instruction himself from members of a company of royal artillery stationed at the Castle; and the train became the school of many good officers of the Revolution. Paddock received two light brass field-pieces, and uniformed a number of German emigrants in white frocks, hair caps, and broadswords, to drag the cannon. These pieces had, it is supposed, been cast in London for the Province from some old cannon sent over for the purpose, and they bore the Province arms. They seem to have been first used when the king's birthday was celebrated, June 4, 1768, in firing a salute, when the train paraded with Colonel

Phips's governor's troop and Colonel Jackson's regiment. At the outbreak of the war these pieces were kept in a gun-house at the corner of West Street; and as Paddock adhered to the royal cause, and might surrender them to Gage, they were stealthily removed by some young Patriots and, on a good opportunity, conveyed by boat to the American camp where they did good service then and through the war; and in 1788 Knox, then secretary of war, had them inscribed with the names of Hancock and Adams, and they now may be seen in the summit-chamber of Bunker Hill Monument. (Drake's *Knox*, p. 127.) The young men who accomplished their removal were, among others, Abraham Holbrook, Nathaniel Balch, Samuel Gore, Moses Grant, and Jeremy Gridley. (Tudor's *Life of Otis*, p. 452.) Judge Story's father was another. (*Life and Letters of Judge Story*, i. 9. See also *N. E. Hist. and Geneal. Reg.* vii. 139.) The committee of safety, Feb. 23, 1775, instructed Dr. Warren to ascertain what number of Paddock's men could be depended on. Drake, *Cincinnati Society*, p. 543, gives a partial list of the train-members, designating such as subsequently served in the Patriot army. Paddock left Boston with Gage, and died in the Isle of Jersey in 1804, aged seventy-six. Mills and Hicks's *Register*, 1775, gives a statement of the Boston military at this time. See Frothingham's *Siege of Boston*, p. 49. — ED.]

[3] [Andrews records, Sept. 5, 1774, that Gage began to build block-houses and otherwise repair the fortifications at the Neck, but he could get none of the artisans of the town to help him. Three days later Gage, "with a large parade of

and Salem the Governor had scarcely any power. The people of the interior counties recognized only the authority of the committees of correspondence, and of the congresses composed of their own representatives.

On the fifth of October, the members of the Massachusetts Assembly appeared at the court-house in Salem, but were refused recognition by

MRS. JOSEPH WARREN.[1]

Gage; thereupon they resolved themselves into a Provincial Congress and adjourned to Concord, where, on the eleventh, two hundred and sixty members, representing over two hundred towns, took their seats, and elected

attendants," surveyed the skirts of the town opposite the country shore, supposably for determining on sites of batteries. See an editorial note to the chapter following this. In November, 1774, Nathaniel Applet on writes to Josiah Quincy, Jr.: "The main guard is kept at George Erving's warehouse in King Street. The new-erected fortifications on the Neck are laughed at by our old Louisburg soldiers as mud walls." *Life of Josiah Quincy, Jr.*, p. 175.—ED.]

[1] [She died in 1773, aged 26. The *Boston Gazette* of May 3 published some commemorative verses on her. Frothingham's *Warren*, p. 228. This painting is the pendant of that of General Warren, and the two have always been owned together.—ED.]

John Hancock president, and Benjamin Lincoln secretary. They sent a message to the Governor, remonstrating against his hostile attitude. He answered by making recriminations; and shortly after issued a proclamation denouncing them as "an unlawful assembly whose proceedings tended to ensnare the inhabitants of the Province, and draw them into perjuries, riots, sedition, treason, and rebellion." The Congress, having adjourned to Cambridge, adopted a series of resolves providing for the creation of a "committee of public safety,"[1] — a sort of directory empowered to organize the militia and to procure military stores.[2] A committee of supplies was also appointed, and three general officers — Preble, Ward, and Pomeroy — were chosen by ballot. Thus the people of Massachusetts proceeded in a calm and statesmanlike manner to organize themselves into an independent existence, and to make suitable provision for their own political, financial, and military necessities. They had no intention of attacking the British troops, but took measures to defend themselves in case of necessity.[3] Hitherto they had carefully avoided being the aggressors, and they were determined to adhere to this policy; but they considered it the part of wisdom to be prepared for any emergency which might arise in the present complicated state of affairs. Consequently, all the towns were advised to enroll companies of Minute Men, who should be thoroughly drilled and equipped.[4]

Gage also on his part was actively employed in strengthening the garrison, and by the end of the year he had no less than eleven regiments, with artillery and marines, quartered in Boston, besides a large number of ships of war at anchor in the harbor. During all this time the Tory party was endeavoring, without much success, to secure adherents to the royal cause.[5] Most of their leaders, finding their position uncomfortable in the

[1] Hancock, Warren, and Church were the Boston members.

[2] [Mr. C. C. Smith contributed a valuable paper on "The Manufacture of Gunpowder in America," to Mass. Hist. Soc. Proc., March, 1876. — Ed.]

[3] [It was at the Green Dragon Tavern, which stood on what now makes Union Street, near where it runs into Haymarket Square (there is a doubt whether the building now marked with a dragon on a tablet gives correctly the site), and whose earlier history is noted in Vol. II., Introduction, p. v, that the leading Patriots held their conclaves. It was in front a two-story brick building with a pitch roof, but of greater elevation in the rear; and over the entrance an iron rod projected, and upon it was crouched the copper dragon which was the tavern's sign. It was probably selected as a meeting place because Warren was the Grand Master of the Grand Lodge of Masons, who had their quarters here. Paul Revere records how he was one of upwards of thirty men, chiefly mechanics, who banded together to keep watch on the British designs in 1774-75, and met here. The old building disappeared in October, 1828, when the street was widened to accommodate the travel to Charlestown. Shurtleff, Description of Boston, p. 605. — Ed.]

[4] [The last monthly meeting of the Friends was held in Boston in the eleventh month of 1774. "The record speaks of its being a time of difficulty in Boston on account of the present calamity [the war]; and the same likely to attend them through the winter, Boston monthly meeting is dropped." — An Historical Account of the various Meeting-houses of the Society of Friends in Boston, published by direction of the Yearly Meeting, Boston, 1874. — Ed.]

[5] See Sabine's Loyalists.

country towns, took refuge in Boston as a kind of asylum. Their organs denounced the Patriots as rebels, rioters, republicans, and sowers of sedition.

At the beginning of the year 1775 the American question was brought forward in the House of Lords by the Earl of Chatham, who, in one of his most eloquent speeches, urged the immediate removal of the king's troops from Boston. He eulogized the American people, their union, their spirit of liberty, and the wisdom which marked the proceedings of their Congress.[1] He charged the ministry with misleading the king and alienating the affections of his subjects. Chatham was ably supported by Shelburne, Camden, and Rockingham; but all their appeals "availed no more than the whistling of the wind." The motion was rejected by nearly four to one. This result, following as it did the rejection by the Cabinet of the petition of Congress which Franklin had just presented, was sufficient proof that nothing was to be hoped for from that quarter. If any further evidence was wanted, it was soon found in the instructions which were sent to Gage to act offensively, and in the Restraining Act, which excluded New England from the fisheries.[2]

While England was thus forcing on the issue, America was preparing to meet it. The new Congress convened at Cambridge in February, and appointed its committee of safety and the delegates to the next Continental Congress. Provision was also made for the militia; and Colonels Thomas

and Heath were commissioned additional general officers. "Resistance to tyranny!" was now the watchword for Massachusetts. "Life and liberty shall go together! Continue steadfast!" said the Patriots; "and with a proper sense of your dependence on God, nobly defend those rights which Heaven gave and no man ought to take from us."[3]

[1] [See the *History of Lord North's Administration*, p. 187; Hugh Boyd's *Miscellaneous Works*, i. 196; *Annual Register*, 1775, p. 47; Belsham's *Great Britain*, vi. 91; *Life of Josiah Quincy, Jr.*, p. 318. — ED.]

[2] [See various references for political movements in England at this time in Winsor's *Handbook*, p. 23, etc. — ED.]

[3] [In March came the anniversary of the massacre, and Warren's most famous address in commemoration. See Mr. Goddard's chapter. The diary of Joshua Green, making note of it, speaks of the attempts of British officers present at the town-meeting which followed, to break it up by unseemly disturbances. (*Mass. Hist. Soc. Proc.*,

1875, p. 101.) About this time (March 22, 1775), according to statements printed in a Boston letter in the *New York Journal*, a number of drunken British officers set to hacking the fence before Hancock's house; and on a repetition of such annoyances, Hancock applied for a guard. While the congregation of the West Church were observing a fast, drums and fifes were played by another party close under the windows. Something of the feeling of the time can be gathered from letters of Quincy, Cooper, Winthrop, and Warren, printed in *Massachusetts Historical Society's Proceedings*, June, 1863, — all addressed to Benjamin Franklin in London. — ED.]

Gage did his utmost to disarm and disperse the militia and seize their military stores. He sent expeditions to Marshfield and Jamaica Plain and Salem;[1] but the judicious and spirited conduct of the inhabitants defeated his object, and the peace was not then disturbed. For a time it was quiet, but it was only the lull before the storm; and the hour of the American Revolution, which had been so long in coming, was near at hand. The War of Independence on this continent began[2] at last on that memorable morning, enshrined forever in the annals of freedom, when

> " The troops were hastening from the town
>   To hold the country for the Crown :
>   But through the land the ready thrill
>   Of patriot hearts ran swifter still.
>
> " The winter's wheat was in the ground,
>   Waiting the April zephyr's sound ;
>   But other growth these fields should bear
>   When war's wild summons rent the air."

*Edward G. Porter*

---

[1] [The expedition to Salem was sent by Gage in transport from the Castle, and its three hundred troops, landing at Marblehead, marched to Salem to seize some cannon. Their failure and retreat is described in Charles M. Endicott's *Leslie's Retreat at the North Bridge, Feb. 26, 1775*, printed separately for vol. i. of the *Essex Institute Proceedings*. See also *Life of Timothy Pickering*, i., and George B. Loring's *Address* on the centennial observance of the event. The contemporary accounts of the Marshfield expedition are in Force's *American Archives*. Of another and more secret expedition just now, that of Captain Brown and his companion De Bernière, sent by Gage inland toward Worcester to pick up information, we have their own account, printed in the *American Archives*, i. Gage's instructions

to these emissaries, Feb. 22, 1775, were printed in Boston in a pamphlet in 1779, which also contains "The Transactions of the British troops previous to and at the Battle of Lexington," as reported to Gage. — ED.]

[2] [Various claims have been made for earlier shedding of blood and resistance in arms, like the capture of the fort at Great Island, near Portsmouth, Dec. 13, 1774, — see *American Archives*, Belknap's *New Hampshire*, Amory's *General Sullivan* and *Governor Sullivan*, *Mass. Hist. Soc. Proc.*, March, 1875; or the Golden Hill affair, Jan. 19, 1770, near New York, — see *Hist. Mag.*, iv. 233, and again January, 1869; or the Westminster massacre, March, 1775, in Vermont, — see *Hist. Mag.*, May, 1859; see also *Potter's American Monthly*, April, 1875. — ED.]

www.ingramcontent.com/pod-product-compliance
Lightning Source LLC
Chambersburg PA
CBHW022150020726
47496CB00008B/2652